S0-DTB-005

BITTER WATER

An Intriguing Historical Novel
Of the Life and Times of Mary

By

Charles William Popell

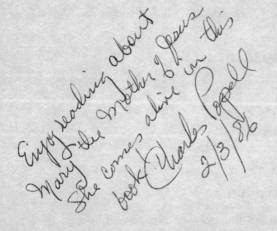

MASTER BOOK PUBLISHERS
SAN DIEGO, CALIFORNIA
92115

BITTER WATER

Copyright © 1984 Charles W. Popell

MASTER BOOK PUBLISHERS, A Division of CLP
P. O. Box 15908
San Diego, California 92115

Library of Congress Catalog Card Number 84-60870
ISBN 0-89051-097-0

Cataloging in Publication Data

Popell, Charles W
  Bitter water.

  I. Title.

813

ISBN 0-89051-097-0   84-60870

Cover by Colonnade Graphics, El Cajon, CA

Printed in the United States of America

Foreword

In his delightful novel, *Bitter Water,* Charles Popell incorporates a wealth of information and depicts a deep insight into his subject which he has garnered in his service for God in a great variety of ways.

As a Biblical scholar, having spent some time in the Holy Land, and ably conversant with the history, culture, geography, and religious traditions of that land of Israel, he provides the appropriate backdrop for the Incarnation, that mighty miracle of the ages.

Because he has experienced being a pastor, Navy chaplain, and intimate counselor to people from every segment of society with every type of problem, his is a competency and a capability to make the characters in the story come alive before the reader's eyes.

The author's experience as an educator, moreover, has provided him with the necessary literary and communication skills to capture and to hold one's interest throughout the narrative. He focuses attention on the mother of our Lord from the moment of the angelic announcement of her supernatural pregnancy until she delivers at full term at the close of the book.

This is a poignant account of an unwed teenager questioning all that is happening within herself and around her. Mary can be accepted as an ideal role model for young and old as she copes firmly with the stresses which are our common lot. Emotional trauma was bitter and baffling for her as it is for us. We identify with her anguish of heart, her fears, her anxieties, her hurting caused by the failure of her nearest and dearest to understand her situation as it actually was.

Young people in our world are frequently forced to make hard choices. Charles Popell portrays Mary as having to make them likewise. When she did, they were always exemplary, although they could have been otherwise. Before her were the options of surrendering to the negative drives of finding easy ways out by abortion or illicit relationship, especially when loved ones and community proved to be harshly judgmental. Her decisions were right because they were based on maintaining faith in God, thus fulfilling His plan for her life while awaiting his ultimate vindication of her yieldness to his control.

As I read *Bitter Water,* always anxious to see the next page, I found "my heart strangely warmed," to borrow the words of John Wesley. There must be something of God in the medium that brings me to a common meeting ground with the author, whose Catholic background is so different from my own.

It is my pleasure to commend enthusiastically this Biblical novel to young and old and to all religious faiths.

—Rev. John S. Burgar
Former Pastor
First Baptist Church
La Mesa, California

Preface

In the growing-up years of long ago, I wondered if Mary, the girl from Nazareth in Galilee, who mothered Jesus, was the kind of person I could fall in love with. Hastily, I'd dismiss the thought with, "Oh well, she belongs to God!—Leave her alone!" In that sense she belonged to many, but to no one in particular. I have changed my mind.

It borders on the sacrilegious to write that Mary, the mother of Jesus, could have succumbed to an abortion while carrying her unborn son. Yet, in fact, her life and times show that the circumstances external to her person were stark. In the "Angel Story," when she was told about how she became pregnant, it is made clear that she was free in every respect; asked by Gabriel whether she would be the mother of Jesus, she replied: "Let what you have said be done to me" (Lk. 1:38). Thereafter, as well, she continued to be completely free.

Tradition has had its hot and cold periods of devotion to Mary. The present generation of believers, confronted with the vagaries of modern sexual behavior, dislikes sham and pretense in human relationships, with the result that the plastic and chalk virgin has been dethroned, or in a more humane way, just merely considered unimportant. Our story is a search for the real Mary.

When Mary's parents discovered that their fifteen-year-old daughter was pregnant and that her fiance was not the father (Mt. 1:25), they quickly hurried her off to their cousins' home in the suburbs of the metropolis, Jerusalem. To remain in the small town of Nazareth and be victimized by gossip would mean death, death by stoning (Dt. 22:20). The Judaic Law would indeed effectively "abort" both the mother and the child from the community.

The Bible gives us many cogent facts about the mother of Jesus, mostly in the Gospels of Matthew and Luke: how she became pregnant not being married; why she left her hometown twice; how she was accused of adultery and faced divorce. Did she run? Was she brave? Under which circumstances would I love her the most?

While in the big city, Mary seemingly enjoyed a sense of anonymity. Did the thought of finding a way out of her burdensome difficulty become a temptation to this young unwed teenager? Jesus in his adulthood, the Son of God, was tempted three times as described in the Bible. Mary, although favored by God, was totally human (Lk. 4).

At the age of thirty-three, Jesus was crucified. At half that age, Mary was threatened with being stoned to death (Dt. 22:20). Her providential survival gave us the Messiah. In order to tell the story of her survival, we researched the times and the culture which bore down heavily upon her and her people.

This tough little girl from Galilee was not a mere tool in the left hand of God that he would hammer into submission. She pronounced her *fiat* to His messenger with determination to be an instrument prepared for service above self. From His high vantage point, God made His choice in the light of human history. Mary was the product of the growth and development of the Jewish people, the human strain of blood chosen and protected by God to formulate the young maiden Mary who accepted the task.

I find it hard to love a "mediatrix" or a "co-redemptrix," as the mother of Jesus has been categorized by some theologians, and the term "Queen of Angels" frightens me! On the other hand, when I find her poor, wearing no ornaments or fancy clothes, but just a plain see-through heart revealing her precious inner self, I can join her friends and neighbors of Nazareth in the song of the day:

> Neither rouge nor powder,
> Neither cream nor scented oil;
> She has nothing artificial about her,
> She is as clean as a doe!
> (author unknown)

Our story, therefore, covers the time of Mary's life only from the moment of her pregnancy to the time of the birth of her baby, the Messiah. It tells of her innermost thoughts and feelings, which she harbors in anticipation of Bethlehem. The very young and the very old love a story, and everyone else will learn with delight and human interest of the stark reality of her motherhood.

There are numerous references to the Bible throughout the book which are directed to the Jerusalem Edition, acceptable to all faiths, published by Doubleday & Co., New York City, New York, for which acknowledgment is herewith given.

—Charles W. Popell

Contents

LIST OF ABBREVIATIONS
FOR BOOKS OF THE BIBLE

Genesis	Gn.
Leviticus	Lv.
Numbers	Nb.
Deuteronomy	Dt.
First Kings	IK.
Psalms	Ps.
Song of Songs	Sg.
Jeremiah	Je.
Isaiah	Is.
Ezekiel	Ez.
Daniel	Dn.
Micah	Mi.
Matthew	Mt.
Mark	Mk.
Luke	Lk.
John	Jn.
Romans	Ro.

Chapter 1

Mary and her unborn baby did not find peace in the big city as she and her worried parents anticipated after she left the small gossipy town in the hill country of Galilee. The murderous King Herod, his henchmen, and the Temple guards were pressing in on her secret, and it was planned to bring her in and break her.

Although Mary felt secure in the comfortable home of her cousin, Zachary, four miles west of Jerusalem, the old Priest nevertheless knew that the sand in the hour glass was running out. He faulted himself for the surge of anxiety that was cresting among the clergy about the imminent birth of the Messiah. Would his birth disturb their life style?

When word first reached the tyrant Herod, it shook his innards into frenzy: "Another rival!" he shouted repeatedly throughout the palace. It meant no more for him to kill a mother and her unborn than it would to crush a nest of vipers that threatened his being. He had already disposed of a few wives, sons, relatives, strangers, and whatever posed a threat to his throne. Now he was searching for the mother of the unborn Messiah.

After three months of befriending his pregnant teenaged Cousin Mary, Zachary felt his inadequacy. His position at the Temple was reduced to insignificance since he had lost his voice. Prior to that, he was held in abjection by his colleagues because of his advanced age and childless marriage. A kind, lovable man was Zachary, but not one to be a Caesar, or even a procurator. His love for Joachim's daughter, his cousin, could make him a martyr, but not a savior.

After Elizabeth delivered their newborn son, John, later to be nicknamed "the Baptizer," Zachary hastened to Mary's room. It was late evening.

"Mary, you must return to Nazareth," said Zachary tiredly. " 'Lizbeth and I have prayed at length over this decision. Be sure you know we love you, but it is no longer safe here for you or your baby."

"When do I leave, Cousin?" asked Mary softly.

"In the darkness of the night, before dawn tomorrow! Aaron shall go with you. He is already making preparations."

"I owe you and Cousin Elizabeth very much!" said Mary. "How shall I ever repay you?"

"Get a good night's rest—as much as you can in what few hours there are left. It'll be a long day tomorrow."

A hush fell over the Zachary household, and the sprawling bedroom suburb slumbered in darkness while Aaron procured the fastest camel in Ain Karim. Only moments after he arrived, Mary was summoned and, taking her meagre belongings, mounted on top of the beast that would take them to Nazareth. Darkness obliterated the tears of parting; sorrow and loneliness came with the tears.

It was much too early and much too dark for Elizabeth and Zachary to do anything more than return to their bedroom. Unceremoniously, the lady of the house slipped under the covers—"still warm" she thought—while Zachary lit the reading lamp next to his chair, placing the Torah on his lap. "Mind if I read you something, 'Lizbeth?" he asked.

"I'm not sleepy—just trying to keep warm."

"It's from Deuteronomy, chapter 22, verse 20, *'But if this charge is true:'* (that is that Mary is not a virgin) *'and*

evidence of the girl's virginity is not found, they shall bring
the girl to the entrance of her father's house, and there her
townsmen shall stone her to death. . . .' "

"What an awful thought!" gasped Elizabeth. "We should
not have let her go. We acted hastily."

"Joseph will disown her," mused Zachary. "The child
she carries is not his. She is now a little over three months
pregnant."

"I know all this, Zachary! Why do you bring it up now?"
Nervously, Elizabeth sat up.

"It seemed like she was snatched from us. I wasn't ready
for her leaving. Sure, we prayed, but I had it in mind to
study the Law before letting her go."

"When will you learn to light the candles before the service! I thought we both knew the Law—and Mary does too."

"I explained to her that 'betrothal' in our Law was the
same as marriage, except that they weren't living together."

"She must be saturated with all that legalism, Zachary,"
said Elizabeth. "You have told her this at the betrothal, and
now again, and again—and still she is galloping with Aaron
into the jaws of the unmerciful beast of small town gossip
that waits for her in Nazareth."

"Deuteronomy here equates betrothal with marriage when
it says in chapter 22, verse—"

"No more, Zachary! Please—I believe that just as Yahweh
saw to it that John was born of me, so will the Messiah be
born of Mary. You must be a believer, husband! Or you'll
lose your voice again."

"It's just that I feel so helpless. . . ."

Chapter 2

A tiny speck found its way from the vastness of heaven to a place near the heart of a mere mortal who bore the ordinary Galilean name of Mary. The mortal and the speck would grow together and become a favored mother and a super Son. As the speck hovered before her face, Mary saw it increase in size emitting a silver brightness. A slender trail of gleaming light seemed attached, no longer than a stylus. Then she felt it enter into her heart, leaving her frightened and spent.

Now four days later, this teenaged, unwed girl began to feel a sense of insecurity and abandonment which shook her entire being. What was she to do with the experience as it grew within her? People would notice her condition. She thought she heard her father say "Chometz" when she left the house that morning to go for water. Her father had used the word repeatedly as he prepared the family for the observance of Passover. It was a tradition of long standing that all the things around the house, foodstuffs, etc., that did not pertain to the Passover, would be sold or given away to people not of their race. It was done to teach the Jewish family that much had to be left behind by their ancestors when they were liberated from Egypt.

"Would the daughter of Joachim," thought Mary, "be separated from her family and her race?" She placed her hand over her abdomen saying, "Chometz."...After a pause, she made it the endearing, diminutive "Chometzla." Love made them one. She prayed, "Help me Lord always to remember that nothing will happen to me that you and Chometzla together can't handle."

Thought triggers emotion, and emotion tugs at the heart, especially when the thought is in the heart of a fifteen-year-old who keeps saying, "I have no one to share my secret!"

"My mother will listen," thought Mary, "but what can she do?...My father? He'll get mad—only Yahweh knows what he'll do!" Her folks had a small olive grove on the outskirts of Nazareth and were looked upon as simple peasants, or in the language of the day, "am-ha-arez," the unlearned country people.

As Mary walked along the white stucco wall approaching the village well, the rays of the rising sun cast strange and prismatic shadows that made her feel awesome and prophetic. At one time the water pitcher on her head became a part of her person and made her look Bedouin and unreal; another time, her abdomen protruded so largely, she said aloud, "The messenger did not say how long it would take."

She was startled! " 'Morning, Mary." It was the low-pitched voice of her friend, Rebecca, who was just about to leave the well.

"Please don't leave, Becky," pleaded Mary.

"Something wrong?" She set her pitcher aside.

"You're just the one I want to see," continued Mary almost breathlessly. "You're sent by God."

Rebecca put her arm around Mary in her usual maternal manner, and since she was quite a bit older this came easily. The two girls sat down in a corner of the well enclosure.

"Everything happens because God wants it to," said Rebecca, using a phrase to which she was accustomed and sincerely believed.

"Becky," began Mary. "I've confided in you before, and

I know you can keep a secret, like when I told you I noticed that I was becoming a grownup woman. You were kind to me.''

''I remember—and you were as nervous as a turtle dove hiding from a hawk. But now, you seem even worse.''

''Promise me you won't tell anyone—nobody—right?''

''Never seemed necessary to promise like this before.''

''Beck, I'm going to have a baby....I'm—''

''So-o, you are solemnly given to Joseph,'' Rebecca noted. ''Everyone in town knows this—It'll only mean that you are now living together.''

''Joseph had nothing to do with it,'' countered Mary.

''Was it someone I know?''

''Becky, it was the Holy Spirit of Yahweh, right after Angel Gabriel told me it was to happen. He came down and into me, and it was total.''

''How long ago did this happen?'' Rebecca looked at Mary's abdomen carefully and with anxiety.

''It was only four days ago,'' replied Mary, ''but being that he is 'the Son of God,' as Gabriel said, I don't know how long it will take.''

''Mary, do you realize that you're not the only girl in Israel who claims to be mothering the Messiah?'' Rebecca was most serious. ''How will your parents take this, when they hear that Joseph is not the father? How about Joseph? What about our well-known vicious villagers? Mary, you must tell your mother—''

''Becky, it frightens me. Look, I'm shaking.''

Rebecca once again put her arms around Mary warmly, assuringly, saying, ''This is God's doing, and He will care for you and your baby. Trust Him. He'll give you the grace of courage when you need it.''

''Dear God,'' prayed Mary, ''I am entirely in your hands. Take me completely and do with me what you will—I pray only that I have the strength to—''

''Well, look at you two,'' came a high, clattering voice. ''Not interrupting anything, am I?'' It was the ratty Sarah come to fetch water.

''Sure,'' said Rebecca, ''but what can we do about it?'' She turned to Mary, saying, ''See you later,'' and departed.

Sarah started filling her pitcher, as Esau her brother and Ruth their sister came charging in.

"Say, Mary, did you hear what happened to Miriam last night?" asked Sarah. "It was awful—"

"Haven't heard," replied Mary, not too interested, for Sarah loved to gossip. She too began to fill her water container.

"You know she is the tanner's daughter—she was found dead at the foot of East Cliff early this morning."

"She was," broke in Ruth. "Why didn't you tell me before?"

"I'm not even telling you now," snapped Sarah. "I'm telling Mary."

"Poor Miriam," said Mary. "Was it an accident?"

"They found a note in her hand," continued Sarah, "and it said she couldn't live any more because the father of her unborn baby left her and ran away."

"Oh no!" gasped Mary.

"You know of course that she wasn't married," said Sarah almost gleefully. "It was an awful thing to do."

"You mean jump off the cliff?" said Mary.

"No, not that so much as what she did with a man before she jumped."

Mary could stand no more. She excused herself, swinging the pitcher atop her head and was on her way. "Yahweh Sabbaoth," she prayed, "did Miriam know what she was doing? And, Lord, protect your Son against my weaknesses—once I thought I could be the greatest mother, but the kind of mother you want me to be now was far from my mind. I never thought about this kind of problem, but it's always like that—dreams don't solve problems!"

Mary prayed as she went down the twisting path homeward. It was a little easier going downhill, as it always is, but the fears arising from Chometzla's presence and the enlarged abdomen on the stucco wall passed her by once more before she reached home.

"Mama!" she cried as she opened the door. "Where are you?"

"Here in the garden," responded Anna. "What's wrong?"

Mary set down her pitcher, ran to her mother, and embraced her. For a prolonged moment she clung to her and then sighed relief.

"Whatever it is, my child, it'll have to wait. Your father is waiting for you—the pigeons must be starving. Be on your way—the bag of grain is just outside the door."

Anna was a rugged old soul, weather-beaten and indifferent to the slings of nature and man. She spoke straight from the heart without the incumbrances of major and minor premises for her conclusions. Hers was the magic of intuition and sentiment. She just knew. That was it. It was this kind of openness that invited friendship with her daughter, Mary. One of Anna's favorite expressions was, "The truth shall make you free—and that too was free!" But it seemed to do more for her than for others.

Mary hurried through the olive grove until she came to the huge mound of rock on top of which was the crudely-structured pigeon loft. Joachim was waiting—but patiently.

"Papa, are you waiting for me," asked Mary demurely, "or for the bag of grain?" She laughed a little.

"Ah, for you, my sweet," said Joachim. "The pigeons are waiting for the grain. Be careful, let no harm befall you, Mar-ree." He pronounced her name in the diminutive, rhyming with "key," and rolling the "r" in the usual Galilean gutteral sound. "Want to see something?" he asked. "Alexander here just this minute returned from Cousin Zachary's." He cupped the champion carrier into his hands, then deftly lifted the goose quill from his leg. He took from it a piece of practically weightless parchment called "duksystos" by the merchants, and was about to read the message. "What's wrong, Mar-ree? Why the gasp'?" asked Joachim distracted.

"Did you say Alexander just flew in from Ain Karim?" asked Mary from deep within herself.

"No," responded Joachim deliberately, "I said 'from Cousin Zachary's....' Come closer, place your fingers over Alexander's heart! It's beating as fast as a stream of peas into a wooden bowl!"

She didn't say it, but she thought hers was beating even faster. The mention of Zachary and Ain Karim triggered it. She wasn't sure just why, but it felt to her like a bolted door just opened by itself, and it beckoned her to run through. Not to change the subject, but she asked, "Is Alexander your best carrier, Papa?"

"Oh yes, by far. He is the only one who goes both ways—and holds some kind of record between Ain Karim and Nazareth. Imagine, he does it in one hour and forty-two minutes, and it takes almost three days for a human on foot. But what happened to the message?"

"I have it right here," said Mary. "Shall I read it?" Joachim nodded. "All's well—thank God—the miracle of conception continues. Zach is still unable to speak. Love to all—signed Zach."

"With due respect to our cousin the priest, he should not have argued with God's messenger. He's still speechless."

"That was six months ago," said Mary, "when Gabriel told him Elizabeth was to give birth to a son. It was then he was punished for his unbelief."

"How do you know all that?" Joachim was surprised. "Such matters are only for grownups to discuss. Did you mother tell you this?"

"Grownup?" asked Mary looking askance at her father. "Did you forget that I am old enough to be married, to be a wife—and mother?"

"Enough. Now run along and take the message to Mama—Wait! I'll go with you," said Joachim, a little confused. "I'm hungry for one—or more—of Mama's cakes." The long-legged, gaunt but regal Joachim came awkwardly down the slope of boulders and walked beside the little daughter whom he loved dearly. "Mar-ree, after I depart to Abraham's bosom, I want your Joseph to have the pigeons, both the carriers and those I've raised for the table. It'll help you and him to keep in touch with Zachary."

"Oh, yes. Joseph—yes!" stammered Mary. She blinked. Her father seemed far away. "God must love him very much."

As they walked around the olive trees set like military tents in an encampment, thoughts swirled about in their consciousness as if blown by the wisdom of the Holy Spirit. Mary had it on the tip of her tongue to tell her father all about the visit of Gabriel. Joachim had a premonition that she was being bothered by something, and he finally made a start. "Need help, Mar-ree?" he asked.

"I should be helping you, Papa." Mary reached out to take his arm.

"No, no, not that," said Joachim. "You seem worried, and I thought you might want to talk."

"No, thanks, Papa." She again changed the subject. "You said Alexander doesn't know he is carrying a message. I think he does, but he can only tell it to another pigeon."

"Aren't you a funny one?" smiled Joachim. "Must I resort to calling you 'My Little Pigeon' to gain your confidence?"

"The arched limbs of the olive trees," she observed, "hang like willows. Isn't that a sign of a rich harvest this year?"

"Plenty of olives for the household, for oil, food, fuel, and medicine—and also we shall be in a position to barter with our neighbors for wheat, barley, and fish. Galilee, as you may not know, Mar-ree, is better known for grain than olives."

The fruit of the trees was important to Joachim, but what was more important were the trees themselves. Every tenth one belonged to Yahweh Sabbaoth, and he himself was only the steward. The yield of the tenth tree was pressed into a pure, sweet olive oil and delivered to the Temple in Jerusalem. There the priests, knowing its excellent quality, would earmark it "for sacred anointings only." On these occasions Joachim would look up his cousin Priest Zachary and spend a few days with him, either at the Temple or in Ain Karim. Sometimes at parting they would look back at the brief visit, jokingly saying no one had mentioned politics, church, or relatives. Since they both were fanciers of carrier pigeons, it was all pigeon talk. They might even exchange a few birds, or just bring a crate full as a gift. The women folk wouldn't like this limitation of subject matter.

As father and daughter approached the house, Mary stopped at the flower garden and noticed how much taller were the finger-like crocuses pushing through the winter-crusted soil. These early spring harbingers filled the highland forests of the countryside. The smaller shoots were anemone, which covered the floor of the valley north and west of

Nazareth.

"These," said Joachim, "were brought here from far and near by tender loving hands. Remember how our great King David's son, Solomon, sang about these signs of Springtime?

'Come then, my love,
my lovely one, come,
for, see winter is past
the rains are over and gone.
The flowers appear on the earth,
the season of glad songs has come,
the cooing of the turtle dove is heard
in our land...' (Sg. 2:10).

"Well now—that left me breathless," said Joachim as he sat down on a flat stone. Mary countered immediately as was their custom when one quoted a line from the scriptures:

*"The fig tree is forming its first fig,
and the blossoming vines give out their
       fragrance.
Come, then my love,
my lovely one, come."*

"Beautiful, Mar-ree," exclaimed Joachim. "You went right on to the finish of the text."

"But the important part, Papa, is the part that comes before where you started. Young people today are not so much interested in flowers as they are in causes and persons. They're preparing the way for the Coming One to restore the Kingdom of Israel:

'See where he stands
behind our wall;
He looks in at the window,
he peers through the lattice.
My beloved lifts up his voice.
He says to me....'

"Then follows the part you started with 'Come then, my love....' " Mary indeed knew something Joachim didn't know. She was pregnant, and his name was to be "Jesus."

"Aren't you two ever going to get inside this house!" crackled Anna at the door, flailing her arms. "The locust cakes have been on the table so long they're about to come back to life."

    "Joseph comes to take you home tonight." Anna poked into the hot embers in the fireplace. Although she had her back to her young daughter, she obviously was addressing her.

    "I thought he was only coming to dinner," said Mary in surprise.

    "It's been six months since the day of your solemn promise. Why the surprise?"

    "Mama, I'm not ready for tonight. I cannot go!" Mary's look plead with her father lying on the cot.

    "Joseph is family," declared Joachim. "Another day or two won't hurt, and anyway, I think Mar-ree should be the one who decides the exact day. She know best about this.

It's a—a personal matter."

"One thing after another," thought Mary. "When will it be my turn to tell them about my problem?"

"Joseph will not be of legal age," continued Joachim, "until next week. What day is that?"

"Exactly eighteen next week on Wednesday," said Anna.

"How does that suit you, Mar-ree?" asked Papa.

"Just fine, Papa," answered Mary, "if the Holy Spirit approves."

Joachim looked at Anna quizzically, wondering why the strange use of the words "Holy Spirit" when in this house it was "Yahweh" that was called upon. They let it pass.

"What's good for Mar-ree," added Joachim, "is good for Josèph."

"That sounds like a turnabout, Joachim," said Anna. "You used to say, 'What's good for Joachim is good for Anna!' Now we have agreement: the wife should come first."

Mary finished setting the table and now stood back to double check. The round metal plates with turned-up perimeters looked at her with open faces and a smile. They harbored no cares or secrets. The goblets stood upright, yawning, empty-minded, and bored. They needed wine. On the mantle over the fireplace where it was warm, there were four carved bowls full of hardened milk still culturing, but they would be ready in a moment's notice.

It was Joachim, the man of the house, who went to the door when the knock came. Mary stood beside him with a bowl of water and a towel. Joseph bowed and refreshed his hands and then his feet in the well water kept cool since morning. Mary handed him the towel.

The young, stocky woodworker of Nazareth was respected in the Joachim home but never feared, even though he was reputed to have put fear into the hearts of some of his customers at the shop where he was occasionally challenged. His piercing look under fire went through and beyond persons and problems, and with that he wielded authority over himself and others. When someone asked him how much it would cost for a repair job or a new item, he would say, "A just price for the affluent, and a little less for the needy."

In his relationship with God, Joseph's ever-abiding faith was founded on the belief that God who made him had a master plan for him, but as with many people, he had a problem in discovering what God's plan was for him. His search for it was his religion.

"Master of the house! Father of my bride!" said Joseph. "I have a surprise for you. Stay right where you are. It stands just outside the entrance."

He returned carrying a beautiful, high-back chair, and set it down at the head of the table. All gathered around examining the carvings, touching the soft red fabric. "Haven't seen anything like this outside the Temple," said Joachim.

"You have made many things for the house," said Anna, "but this is the greatest. It's beautiful."

"Joseph, your kindness exceeds our merits," said Mary.

"Please take your usual place at the family table," invited Joachim, "and—will you be kind enough to offer the prayer?"

"Who am I to take your place before God?" pleaded Joseph. "This is your home, your table—you are the priest of the moment."

"Let it be," responded Joachim, who loved every word he heard:

"One, Holy and Eternal God! We earnestly beseech you, in this moment of happiness, to bless our new son, Joseph! Bless Mary, our daughter, soon his wife to be.
Bless our table, this home. May we all share the future together, as one family in one God. Amen."

"Joachim, you would make an excellent Rabbi," said Joseph.

"Our tribe is the tribe of David, as you know," said the Master of the house, "and it is meant for kingship, not for the priesthood—but I don't have a chance for either."

"Speaking of David," said Joseph, "the wing of the bird has it that the Messiah is about to be born among us. Not a day passes that some traveler doesn't stop by from some far away place to tell he has heard the new king of Israel is about to be born. It's like some Giant has shouted the news from Mt. Hermon and everybody now knows it at the same time."

"Did you say 'to be born among us'? This can't be. The prophecy says that he will be born in Bethlehem—"

"—And," interjected Anna, "every young Jewish girl who becomes pregnant today makes that claim. It's been going on for twenty years."

"Micah the prophet," continued Joachim, "says, *'But you, Bethlehem, the least of the clans of Judah, out of you will be born for me the one who is to rule over Israel'* (Mi. 5:1). This obviously limits the claims geographically."

"Another limitation," Joseph offered, "is the one mentioned by the great Isaiah that the Messiah shall be born from our stock, the tribe of David" (Is. 11:1 ff.).

Mary suddenly pushed her chair back, stood up, and collected the empty milk bowls, then went to the fire in the garden to bring in the lamb roast. The conversation was disturbing.

As she returned, she heard Papa saying, "I like what Isaiah says about the Messiah's mother, that she shall be very young, a young virgin, or perhaps a recently married young woman. The word he uses is 'Almah'—*'The Almah is with child and will soon give birth to a son'* (Is. 7:14). I understand this to mean virginal conception—"

Hearing this, Mary wasn't sure whether she was carrying the lamb roast, or it was pulling her—she plunked it down in front of Joseph. All eyes were upon her.

"Mar-ree!" exclaimed Papa from his regal perch. "The lamb belongs here—I shall serve it."

"Of course, sorry, Papa," she said as she rallied promptly to the correction. Her mind was racing. She thought of Miriam at East Cliff—if she could only jump into space, run and hide, disappear....Couldn't they talk about something else? The room was full of hideous faces, talking loudly, ridiculing her; some were waving sticks and stones as if to strike—one had a huge two-edged sword! But it was Papa waving his carving knife. Mary sat down.

"From what I've heard at the shop," continued Joseph, "and what has been said by the prophets, the time is ripe for the Messiah. Israel needs him now—or never."

"Not again," thought Mary. "This is not my time to

talk....Immanuel, help me!"

"What have you heard?" pursued Joachim.

"Some of it we all know from the prophets—that the people of God are oppressed by foreigners; Roman soldiers are seen everywhere. Our High Priests are no more; as a result Judaism as religion-and-state-in-one does not exist. The Temple and the government are warring with each other. Many intellectuals, Rabbis for instance, have joined the service of the foreigner. Those who are loyal, such as the Zealots, are being crucified by the hundreds—"

"Don't forget the disapora," added Joachim. "Our Jewish people are now scattered through the world. Why would Yahweh want all this?"

"Most of it," said Anna, "was brought on by the wickedness of our own people. They have not lived by the Covenant." Then she turned directly to Joseph. "Do you believe the time has come for the Messiah?"

"No," mused Joseph, "I don't think we have yet suffered enough."

"I agree with you, Joseph," said Joachim. "If I heard of someone claiming to give birth to the Messiah, I would say it's another delusion, not unlike some of our King Herod's dreams."

Mary could stand it no longer. Again she pushed back her chair, excused herself, and went to the garden. "My God," she prayed, "my own people are unbelievers. Why can't I tell them—and make them believe?" Perhaps she answered her own question, for she heard within herself the words she spoke to Gabriel only a few days ago. "Be it done to me in accord with your word." "I must keep faith with the Holy Spirit," she told herself. "Don't force the issue. Always wait if it's not clear what to do." As she scanned the canopy of the heavens with its flickering stars and felt the massiveness of the darkened hills around her, she wiped away a tear as it hung on the corner of her mouth—

"Mary! Mary!" came the hushed voice of her mother.

"What is it, Mama?"

"Dry your tears, it is enough." consoled Mama as she put her arms around her. "The world will not change for what you did—the roast is just as delicious in front of

Joachim or Joseph—and already half gone."

"It's not really that, Mama," said Mary as she was being led back into the house by her mother. The men were
now having their wine and toasting each other for having
solved the problems of the world.

"Anna, you did a marvelous job on the roast," com-
plimented Joseph, "—and, Mary, the service was excellent."

"Ah, yes," said Joachim, "the aroma of mustard seed
and garlic did indeed gain ascendancy over the
preponderance of onion, and we love them all—almost as
much as we love you two women."

"Words, words, words, Joachim," answered Anna, "but
thank you both."

"Yes, and I have some more words," said Joachim.
"Words of great import to my new son." He poured some
more wine into their goblets. "When you and Mary made
your solemn promise to wed last year at the Temple, you
pledged a certain amount of money as Mohar. All of us in
this house are agreed that this should not be paid, now or
ever. I understand from Anna that you have come to take
Mary home with you tonight."

"I'm ready to offer you the dowry, father of my bride,
and also it is true that I would like Mary to come and start
living with me."

"Mary has asked me to tell you," continued Joachim,
"that it should never be said that you had to pay a price
in money for her."

"Very well," countered Joseph, "but no one can deny
me the privilege of making a gift to Mary, the Mattan. I've
set aside fifty shekels of silver since our engagement" (cf.
Dt. 22:17). "Also, Mary, here is a sash in which you can
hide the gift, if you ever need to."

"Lovely," exclaimed Mary. "Thank you, Joseph."

"Joseph, you have always been most generous to us.
Thanks." said Joachim. "But allow me to pursue the subject further. You will be of legal age to marry only next
Wednesday—and coincidentally it is the proper day
designated for marrying a maiden such as our daughter. This
then makes it impossible for you and your bride to consum-
mate the union tonight according to the words of the book

of Deuteronomy. Hakhnashah must wait until at least Wednesday.''

"Plainly spoken, Joachim," answered Joseph. "I have no intentions of disobeying our laws, especially now that I have a bride like Mary. I accept your decision, however, with disappointment.''

Mary brushed a tear from her cheek. No one but she knew exactly why. The pressure was off now, and she had a few days to tell her mother of the angel's visit.

It was late when Joseph left. "What a night this could have been," he said, almost scornful of the full moon rising swiftly over the Sea of Galilee. "She should be right here, at my side, walking home—I waited a long time for this night." As he walked by East Cliff, a surge of energy passed through his virile frame, so that he compulsively grasped a huge rock and heaved it over the hillside, starting a small avalanche. His frustration subsided.

Meanwhile, Mary thought she felt a tremor reverberate through her bedroom; she thought it was distant thunder, but she heard no more and thought it was strange. She then began to recite the lengthy Shema: the prayers of her forefathers at twilight in which she spoke of the oneness of God. She was distracted by the happenings of the evening, especially when Joseph showed his desire for oneness. She thought of the oneness of her parents—she felt sorry for Joseph. Looking through the window, she saw the goat in an unusually frisky caper. He was rocking on his front and rear legs in a stiff manner.

Sleep was far from her mind, so Mary went on offering all eighteen benedictions, long, repetitious. And when she came to the part about the "Advent of the Kingdom," again her mind wandered. "Would Chometzla," she asked, "grow from a tiny speck to become a king with a long, flowing train? Now he has the small room under my heart. Then will he have a magnificent palace?" She recalled, half in dreamland and half awake, that Gabriel said, *"God will give him the throne of his ancestor David"* (Lk. 1:32). She repeated the benediction about the Kingdom.

"How long will it take him to be born?" she asked.

No one answered.

"Will he be a year old at birth? Mama says an infant is a year old when born."

Still no answer.

"What is God going to tell Joseph?"

June nights are chilly in Galilee. Mary drew the several covers over her head, restlessly searching for that comfortable posture that usually brought sleep. It eluded her. Rebecca told her, she recalled, that some people find sleep when reciting the family genealogy. She fell into the rhythmic cadence:

" *'Abraham was the father of Isaac, Isaac was the father of Jacob, Jacob the father of Judah—and his brothers; Tamar being his mother. . . David the father of Solomon, whose mother. . . . Then the deportation to Babylon took place. . . . After the deportation. . . '*(Mt. 1:1). zzz z z z '. . . .After his birth, give him the name of Jesus. . . . He will rule over the house of Jacob. . . . '*z z z z z z z z z z z z 'Night, Chometzla!''

"I've got to tell Mama," was Mary's first thought the next morning. "I must, I must, I must," she kept saying as she dressed hurriedly. Her usual morning prayers turned into the prayer of spontaneous union with Yahweh God. She saw God walking on stilts of vaporous sunlight through the window, stepping over huge limestones on the distant slope.

Closer to home, she saw Papa striding down the pathway that snaked through the olive grove, heading for the pigeon loft. "It's kind of early to be feeding," she thought, "but this is my chance," and she hurried into the living room.

"Mama, I've been wanting to tell you about what happened to me the other day—"

"Tell me first how you found out that Cousin Elizabeth has been pregnant for six months?" asked Mama.

"It was you who told me she was pregnant," replied Mary.

"I didn't tell you how long."

"No, it was Gabriel who told me that," pleaded Mary, "just five days ago."

"Never heard of the man," said Anna. "What's his

name?''

"He's not a man," said Mary, "—not like Miriam's friend—did you hear what happened to Miriam, Mama?''

"Miriam, the tanner's daughter?''

"Yes, she jumped off East Cliff and was found dead yesterday morning—poor Miriam!''

"Why would she do that?''

"They found a note in her hand, saying she was expecting a child, and she was afraid that the villagers would stone her." Mary kept sweeping the floor.

"Who is the father?" asked Anna. "Where is he?''

"He ran away—Miriam must have been overcome by fear, scared to death...alone...despairing....''

"How would you know all that?" said Mama lightly.

"I'm pregnant, Mama.''

"My God! Yahweh Sabbaoth! Dear girl, you don't know what you're saying!" Anna dropped everything and stood looking at her baby daughter.

"Miriam needed a man," said Mary. "He failed her. I'm not sure what I need right now, except maybe to tell you everything—''

"Start from the beginning, Mary," urged Mama as she took her daughter by the hand and led her into the garden.

"It's difficult to tell, and it's difficult to believe," Mary began. "Last Sabbath, while I was reciting the Benedictions, the room was filled with light, and I heard a voice saying, *'Rejoice, God has favored you...you shall conceive and bear a son, the Son of God'* '' (Lk. 1:26-38).

"Did the voice say who he was?" asked Anna.

"He said he was sent by God, and Gabriel was his name. He spoke very kindly. He didn't make me afraid.''

"Did you see him?" Anna was deliberate.

"No, there was just the bright light and the voice—he told me not to worry that the Holy Spirit would take care of everything.''

"Was there some kind of proof that this was from God?''

"The messenger said 'Cousin Elizabeth is old, yet she too has conceived a son, now in her sixth month. This proves that nothing is impossible with God!' ''

"So that's how you found out about Elizabeth.'' Anna

nodded her head. "Papa will want to know this. He asked me about it last night."

"Mama, do you think he'll believe me?"

"I pray that he will, but how about Joseph? How about the people of Nazareth?"

"Many times the thought has come to me to leave Nazareth," said Mary. Her despair was showing.

"Wait until we talk to your father. Let's see what he says." Anna got up off the bench and walked about in the small area praying the Psalter, *"Give thanks to Yahweh for he is good, his love is everlasting!"* (Ps. 118).

Was her mother in a thankful mood for what had happened? She asked uncertainly: "Mama, do you believe in me?"

"Yes. In you, I believe. But your story will have to stand the test of your father—now, go fetch me the dried locusts and flour, so I can get on with preparing lunch."

The women went about their morning chores in silence and prayer. It was needful to work and easy to pray, but the time dragged on for want of hope and a plan of action. Mary's faith was more secure, for she knew what transpired within her on supernatural grounds, while Mama had it only on the say-so of her teenaged daughter. Yet at this moment both were in the darkness of indecision.

When the sunlight shafted straight down the chimney, forming a square figure on the floor of the fireplace, Anna knew it was lunch time, and the man in her life would be coming through the door. And when the pegs in the large wooden door creaked in their sockets, she knew he was home.

"Must pour a little olive oil into those sockets," he said as he walked toward his new high-back chair and dropped into it. "Thank you, Joseph!" he exclaimed. "That hillside gets steeper each time I climb it."

Mary brought her father a bowl of fresh water for his hands and a towel for drying them. Anna had already set a cup of yesterday's soup before him, a jug of wine, and then brought the big surprise, Papa's favorite locust cakes. "King David never had it better." said Joachim as he slurped his soup with sounds of satisfaction.

"There is sad news abroad," Anna started to say.

"Now, Anna. Why do you always start with telling me nothing!" interjected Joachim. "Why don't you just tell me the news?"

"Mary heard at the well that Miriam jumped off East Cliff. She was pregnant, and the father of her child skipped the country."

"Oh, the ignorance of young girls!" lamented Joachim. "They should be better instructed about babies by their mothers. They should not be so promiscuous. The time for this kind of thing is during marriage!—Mar-ree, pass me the locust cakes...Thanks!"

"How about somebody instructing the young men, Papa?" asked Mary.

"Your Jeremiah-like lamentations come too late for Miriam, Husband," said Anna. "God will judge her."

And with that, Anna seemed to have summoned the God of Judgment, for a long, reverberating roll of thunder came forth from the nearby hollows off the plain of Esdraelon. "Rain clouds," said Joachim. "It's growing unusually dark."

" 'Yahweh has chosen to dwell in the thick cloud!' " quoted Anna (I K. 8:12). And with a sense of intuition, she added, "He comes to speak to us."

Over the rock-ribbed foothills, the rain was already falling. Joachim looked out the window and saw the swirling, heavily-laden clouds moving swiftly toward the sea of Galilee. With the Galileans, if it was a long-awaited rain, they welcomed it by rushing outdoors, lifting their arms heavenward, and letting the rain wash down their faces. They would break into song and dance and work themselves into a frenzy. But it was not like that today. The downpour was heavy on the thatched roof, and it began to leak. Joachim calmly suggested, "Let's all go into the cave storehouse," as he lighted a lamp to carry. The next roll of thunder swept directly overhead, and the limestone walls of the cave shook.

"The God of thunder is washing down the stains of Miriam's death at East Cliff," said Joachim. He sounded like a prophet.

"He might wash down the whole of East Cliff and the rest of us sinners," added Anna, as she gave Mary a go-ahead sign with a nod toward Papa.

All were seated on the floor when Mary began, "Papa, a few days ago, I had a visit in my room from Gabriel, and he—"

"Gabriel? Who is Gabriel?" asked Joachim.

"He said he was a messenger from God," said Mary, "and told me that I was to have a son, and his name—"

"Are you saying that he told you you're pregnant?" asked Joachim. "You haven't been alone with Joseph, have you? Well, I know you haven't!"

"Joachim, calm down." urged Anna. "Listen to Mary's story, the whole of it. There are decisions to be made."

After a moment of silence, Mary again began, "After Gabriel told me I was favored by God, he left me in total darkness. Gradually I saw this tiny light, as if it were in the distance and racing to come close to me. It made its way under the bridge of my folded hands and just below my heart. It passed through my clothing, my skin, my flesh—and lodged inside of me. It spread all over my body. I began to feel bigger than this house. The light coming through the window was no more. The room was dark, and yet, yet, I could see—I could see the light whether my eyes were open or shut."

"It's frightening." Anna shivered. "Did you feel any movement inside you?"

"No, just kind of a gentle warmth and the presence of something bigger than me—"

"Was this forced on you by Gabriel?" asked Joachim.

"No, Papa. I said it happened after he left."

"Did you at any time give consent?" he asked.

"Oh yes, I said, 'Be it done to me as you wish!' Then he said, 'The Holy Spirit will take care of everything.' "

"Everything?" questioned Joachim. "Everything!" he answered himself.

"Papa," asked Mary, "what will Joseph do when he finds out I'm pregnant?"

"Being the man that he is, and not your child's father, he'll disown you, and when he does that, Nazareth will be too small for you."

"—And the Law says," observed Anna, "the villagers have a right to stone her."

"Mar-ree, you can't stay here any longer," decided Joachim, standing up. "You must leave this town."

"Papa," pleaded Mary, "I must ask you one more question. Do you believe my story?"

"Never a doubt. You're too much a part of me."

During the ensuing moments of silence, they listened to their thoughts, the heavy splashing rains on the roof—and the living room floor. They heard the gurgling waters rush outside through the fissures in the earth along the house. The sudden downpour ended. Diminishing sounds of thunder rolled eastward over the Sea of Galilee, and once more beams of sunlight entered the Joachim home.

As they were passing through the living room headed for the outdoors, Anna said, "Joachim, Mary didn't mention it, but it was Gabriel who told her that Cousin Elizabeth was six months pregnant—remember, you wanted to know!"

"That's it," stated Joachim sharply. "That's it. Mary will go to Cousin Elizabeth's—she will be on hand to assist her in her final days before birth. Mar-ree, how soon can you get ready to leave?"

"Whenever you say, Papa." Mary glanced at her mother.

"—And he thought of it all by himself—" whispered Anna to Mary.

"Our Cousin Zachary, familiar that he is with the Temple and the ancient scriptures," continued Joachim, "will advise and encourage you."

"Husband, you have been inspired! Mary can stay in Jerusalem and be completely lost to this world of small town gossipers and vicious people."

"Joseph will be sick with grief when he hears of this," said Mary. "Do you think it'll be possible for him to join me in Jerusalem?"

"How do you think she should travel?" asked Anna.

"I will accompany her," said Joachim. "We will be on our way tomorrow. Right, Mar-ree?"

"Wrong!" interjected Anna. "You're too sick to travel.

You'd be more of a burden than a help."

"It's nice of you to want to go," said Mary.

"Jonathan ben Hannan and his wife Deborrah are making the trip to the Holy City in the next caravan. There may be others, too, from Nazareth," said Anna. "Mary and I will visit them this afternoon."

Joachim shielded his eyes with both hands as the family emerged into the bright sunlight after the storm. The foliage on the olive trees had turned from a dry gray to a sparkling green polished by the rainfall. The parched land with its jigsawed pattern had now become one soft bosom of nature receptive for the new life of springtime. Joachim was pleased with what he saw and raised his long arms as if to encompass his whole plot of land. "Yahweh, let the unborn son be praised!"

"Joachim," nudged Anna, "look at the awful washout near the pigeon loft." The water was still flowing through the wadi, rushing headlong with silt and debris to find its lowest level somewhere in the valley.

"Too much rain in too short a time," commented Joachim. "The pigeons seem safe enough. Mar-ree, when you leave for Zachary's, I wish you would take along Alexander and two others so as to keep us informed. You know we'll be anxious."

"I'll send Alexander first, so that you can return him to Zachary's before I get there," she said.

"Good plan." said Joachim.

That afternoon, while he was taking a brief nap, Anna and Mary slipped away to Jonathan ben Hannan's place. They came upon the master of the house, a distinguished silversmith of middle age, standing knee-deep in mud repairing a drainage ditch. Deborrah, his wife, and their three daughters, who were scattered over the expansive yard collecting debris brought on by the excessive rainfall, gathered around Anna and Mary.

"Our Cousin Elizabeth is expecting," said Anna, "and Mary is going to Ain Karim to stay with her for a while. We wondered if she could travel with you folks—heard you might be leaving tomorrow."

"Wish I could go to the big city!" said Taman, the eldest

girl.

"For you, even Nazareth is too big," said her father. "But, Anna," he turned to his visitor, "we can't travel tomorrow; the wadis are running deep, the rivers are high, there are no bridges. How about the first day after the Sabbath? There is a large caravan coming from Damascus and heading for Alexandria, Egypt."

"We will be much safer in the caravan," assured Deborrah.

"This'll be fine," said Anna. "Tomorrow is a short day, and you would not be traveling on the Sabbath. Mary'll be ready at sunrise on the first of the week."

Early the next morning, Mary started out for the village well as a routine matter. As she approached the massive pile of boulders, however, where she made the turn up the slope, she stopped. She had a feeling that someone was following her. She turned around quickly. There he was—Joseph.

"Couldn't you hear me calling you, Mary? I've been running my lungs dry to catch up with you."

"Sit down, dear man," she said, as she sat next to him, setting her pitcher down in front of her.

"Mary, I haven't been able to sleep, eat, or work since we talked at your house night before last—it's what you said."

"Sounds a bit exaggerated," smiled Mary.

"I just haven't been myself—I keep asking myself, 'Why didn't you want to come home with me after all these months of waiting'?"

Mary hesitated a moment. "Papa and Mama decided that I should go down to Ain Karim to be with our Cousin Elizabeth who is expecting her baby in three months."

"Three months! You mean you're going to be gone three months?"

"I dont know how long it'll be—I'll be willing to come back whenever I must."

"I'm upset thinking about waiting three days, and now you say three months—Mary, you come with me, and I'll see to it that your folks do nothing more about it. You belong to me!"

"Oh, Joseph! Don't make it so difficult! I can't, but I'd

like to. I too have been waiting for months—Don't you believe me?''

"I'd like to think so, and I guess you're right. Maybe I should talk to your father again.'' He stood up as if to leave.

Mary stood up, too. "Joseph, I'd better be on my way, and if Mama asks me why I'm late getting home, I can't tell her that I was delayed by you. Heavens, Papa will come to see you before you even get close to seeing him. 'Bye, Joseph.''

She braced the water jar on her head with her hand as she turned to take a look at him. He hadn't moved at all and kept looking her way. He was too far away to see the tears that fell from her worried face.

The impetuosity of youthful Joseph would have pursued the dreams of Hakhnashah had he not been restrained by the worrisome thought of his commitment to deliver the Naphtir in the Synagogue on the Sabbath. An obligation to take the pulpit before the community gathered in sacred worship caused him many an anxious moment in preparation. The townsfolk were saying that the young carpenter had some special information about the very popular and highly controversial subject concerning the birth of the Messiah.

The Synagogue in Nazareth had little gold and silver; it was mostly made of the austere stone found in the Galilean hills and roughly hewn by their own peasantry who were something less than artisans in these matters. However, it was generally filled with worshippers, and this Sabbath which belonged to Joseph found it overflowing. In keeping with the basic ideology of the Jewish people, monotheism melded their diverse activities, both civic and religious, into oneness. Judaism must be defined as loyalty and service to both God and country simultaneously. Thus the Synagogue in a small town served as a courthouse, the meeting hall, and the church. Loyalty to Yahweh and patriotism are but one virtue.

Every Sabbath brought Nazareth to a standstill, but today the usual complacent routine gave way to an atmosphere charged with the expectation of change. The long finger of the prophets now rested on this moment.

The hour-long liturgy, basically existential, was directed by a master of ceremonies called the "Hazzan," who prepared all things days in advance. He selected seven readers, who read selections from the Law and the Prophets, and an outstanding, capable person to deliver the Naphtir, the good news from Yahweh. Joseph, though young, already had a public image.

On the upper level of the U-shaped building, reserved for women, sat Anna and her daughter Mary, both neatly dressed in their Synagogue best. Divine services generally compel people to self-examination, and today Mary was very much aware of her pregnancy. However, she felt clean, and there was no guilt to haunt her, except her feeling toward Joseph a little. She wrestled with the obligation that he should know...that she needed him to give the child a name...that these same people around her would stone her if she didn't have him. Or, was it to be someone like him? "Dear God," she prayed.

"Blessed are Thou, Yahweh, God of Israel," declared the Hazzan, opening the service loudly and clearly, "the God who formest the light of the world, and who hath promised His people the Messiah to bring salvation from the oppression of the foreigner. Grant us peace in our time."

"Amen." The congregation's answer signalled their full attention.

Then they were directed to stand and recite the creed, the "Shema" in which the God of Israel was extolled as being the only and one God.

After six of the eighteen Benedictions were recited from the Shemoneh Esreh and the seven readings by various persons from the Pentateuch, an awed, restful hush fell over the crowded Synagogue.

A slight disturbance in the gallery was caused by Taman, the eldest of the Hannan girls, who changed seats in order to be seen better by Joseph, now crossing over to the lectern. In spite of the distraction, all eyes were on Joseph, who bowed reverentially toward the Aron, the ark in which were kept the precious scrolls. He was nervous; it was his first Naphtir; he was prepared to make the texts in Hebrew and give the commentary in Aramaic. Quietly invoking the Holy

Spirit, he began:

"Fellow Galileans, friends:

"**Many travelers have stopped by my shop lately telling of the rash of teenaged girls, married and unmarried, who claim to be mothering the Messiah. This phenomenon is rampant throughout Judea, Samaria, and Galilee.**

"**Do not be deceived. The young girl who is the real mother lives in Bethlehem and is a descendant of the royal line of King David. Look to Bethlehem for the true Savior and King of Israel.**

"**Be forewarned that all the prophetic conditions have now been fulfilled in our time.**"

After elaborating these points, Joseph offered the following three Messianic texts in Hebrew, since up to this point he was speaking in the popular language of Aramaic. This was customary in delivering the Naphtir.

"**First: 'The Lord Himself will give you a sign. It is this: the virgin is with child, and soon will give birth to a Son, whom she will call Immanuel' (Is. 7:14).**

"**The second text: 'But you Bethlehem, Ephrathah, the least of the clans of Judah, out of you will be born for me the one who is to rule over Israel' (Mi. 5:1).**

"**Lastly: 'Rove to and fro through the streets of Jerusalem, look, now, and learn, search her squares; if you can find a man, one man who does right and seeks the truth, then I will pardon her, says Yahweh' (Je. 5:1).**"

Once again, Joseph switched back to the Aramaic, the language of the man in the street, to point out how much Israel had disintegrated as a nation and failed in its covenant with God: "**It has been sixty-three years since General Pompey conquered our people and desecrated our temple. No more do the priests of Judaism rule, but we have a half-Jew pagan King Herod who murders his sons and his wife and crucifies his enemies.**

"**Many are the dynamic factions that splinter the one God and His one chosen nation: the Sadducees dominate what's left of the priesthood. The Pharisees in a two-faced manner oppose King Herod and compromise with the Roman oppressor. The Herodians have not only sold out to the Romans, but have taken on the culture of the Greeks.**

"Another smaller group of our people, although gifted with the grace of the Holy Spirit, has separated itself from the action and gone to the desert to seek a monastic life. They are the Essenes of Qumran. They cry 'repentance' but there is no one in the wilderness to hear their voices.

"And, lastly, the Zealots of Galilee. Are we hastening the birth of the Messiah with revolution and destruction? Are we preparing his way by reducing all things to a flux, to a nakedness of man, to the ashes of negatives?

"Fellow Galileans, friends, Israel is no more! It has already been destroyed, from within and from without. Let it not be said that 'nothing good comes from Galilee,' but let us present to God and to our beloved fatherland a positive good that will save us and all of Israel.

"Let us find the Messiah."

There was a profound sincerity in the voices of the congregation this day in Nazareth as they sang from the Psalter "The Lord is My Shepherd" as a recessional. Mary said to her mother, "Joseph was inspired."

"I hope he will be inspired," said Anna, "when his challenge comes."

They made their way through the crowd to the side door where Joseph was already surrounded by admirers commenting about his Naphtir.

Taman, first one out, though usually last one in the Synagogue, was saying, "Congratulations, Joseph. Who is the lucky girl to be chosen the mother of the Messiah?"

"It's nice to see you interested." Joseph was dubious.

"Good to hear you say the future belongs to the young," commented Houle.

"Did I say that?" he remarked. "I do believe in it, though."

After Mary and Anna exchanged greetings with Joseph, Mary said, "We're leaving with the caravan tomorrow morning for Jerusalem, and from there to Cousin Elizabeth's in Ain Karim."

The situation was awkward, but Joseph easily managed a look of deep concern.

"Cousin Elizabeth," Anna said, "is expecting, and we all agreed at home that Mary should go down to help her.

Hope you don't mind?"

"Of course I do," he replied. "When will she be back?"

"I don't know for sure, Joseph, but as soon as possible," said Mary.

"You're not going alone?" he asked.

"No, I'll be with the Hannans all the time."

Joseph wanted to pursue his questioning to get to the bottom of this sudden turn of events, but the crowd increased, and Mary and her mother disappeared down the hillside toward home.

"Mama, why can't we tell Joseph the whole truth?" asked Mary, bewildered. "He's a part of the family."

"He may stop you from going." But Anna was not too sure of herself. "It just isn't God's will," she added with finality.

Mary fought off a surge of self-pity brought on by the thought of never seeing Joseph again, of shattered dreams about having a home of her own and a family. As she recalled the frightening conditions Joseph described in his Naphtir, especially prevalent in Jerusalem, her sense of insecurity grew acute, and her loneliness possessed her. She fell victim to her worrisome thoughts and began to search within herself for the one who the angel said was to be called "Jesus."

Chapter 5

A night without sleep gradually yielded to the light of the sun ushering in the first day of the week.

"Put the crate of pigeons on the lead donkey," Mary heard Jonathan telling Joachim.

Mary was ready physically to leave, but her sentimental attachment to her room was strong. She stood—"for the last time," in her favorite spot looking through the window, saying farewell to every living thing, and to each little star as it withdrew from the light of the new day. She knelt down on the place in the corner where it all happened just seven days ago. "Hold my hand," she prayed to the Holy Spirit, "and take me and Chometzla wherever you wish."

Then she suddenly turned and left. Outside she stood next to Jonathan, who was adjusting the load under the pigeon crate. After she greeted him, she noticed through an accidental opening in the rolled carpet several glistening points of polished iron. "Sica, daggers," she thought, "the kind Papa and Joseph talked about which identify Zealots." She said nothing and went about her business. She rushed to embrace Mama and Papa to bid them farewell. "Papa, I hope my leaving is the right thing to do—there seems so much to lose and so little to gain by it."

"Now, now, don't worry," said Joachim. "We discussed all that. Remember the father of your child is not a visible human creation, and he therefore will not act like the usual father—or husband. But, He *will act*. He will care for you both."

When Mary kissed her mother and they hugged tenderly, tears began to flow freely. There was an ominous moment of silence—which prompted Joachim to remark, "Rain need not be accompanied by thunder!" They laughed through the sadness of parting. Jonathan and Deborrah and the three donkeys were disappearing over the crest, and Mary hastened to join them, turning back to wave just once more. Then she too disappeared into the unknown.

The huge caravan had already begun to untangle itself from the bundles of the night and was stretching from head to tail on the dew-covered floor of the valley. Thoughts of home faded quickly as strangers, camels, carts, soldiers, and people—just many people—jostled into position. Suddenly, a sharp, gutteral voice cracked through the foggy stillness of dawn. It came from over the crest. "Hold on! Wait a minute," it rang out.

All eyes turned back to the top of the hill. It was a man. Mary immediately recognized Joseph, his gait and stubby arms swinging.

"If you don't mind," said Joseph, "I'm going to walk you to the caravan." He relieved Mary of her traveling bag.

"What brought this on?" asked Mary.

"I forgot to tell you yesterday after services that I love you."

"How sweet is the visible human creature," she murmured.

"What do you mean? I don't understand."

"Someday, I hope, it'll all be made clear for you."

"Right now would be better."

"But, Joseph, the caravan is already moving, and Jonathan is waving madly for me to catch up."

Men on horseback were speedily riding back and forth from head to tail of the caravan, shouting instructions and asking questions. The train was dragged out already for half a mile, headed by a sumptuously bedecked carriage drawn by four Arabian roans, typical of a Roman emissary. Another followed a short distance, less military but more opulent with several wagons and scores of camels heavily loaded. Joseph told Mary this was an affluent merchant, and with all this she would be well protected.

Out of nowhere came a horseman and halted before Joseph and Mary, shouting "Move along farther back with the am-ha-arez, the rest of the Galilean peasants!"

"Don't push!" cried Joseph.

"Let's go back," urged Mary.

"Sorry, we have orders from the head carriage," said the solider.

"And who is that?" asked Joseph.

"Not that it matters here," said the soldier, "but he is an emissary from Caesar Augustus, Vitellius by name—now, move it!...But, just a moment." He peered sharply from under his headgear, then gracefully turned his prancing horse close to Mary. "Haven't seen anything as nice in a million cities," he smiled. "Where did you get the healthy tinted pomegranate cheeks, Venus?" he asked of Mary.

"Go easy, brother," interjected Joseph, as Mary clutched his arm.

"Are you from Nazareth?" asked the rider of Mary.

"Yes," said Joseph. "He means no harm," said Mary.

"At last something good has come from Galilee!" shouted the rider as he jerked the bridle and jumped away.

"That dirty-minded pagan," said Joseph, spitting after him. He then turned to Mary and excitedly began admonishing her in a most paternal manner to stay away from such clap-trap and remain at all times with the Hannans. Mary smiled at her fiance's solicitude.

People and their impedimenta began to move more briskly down the road through the valley of Jezreel, following in the footsteps of the sons of Abraham, Isaac, and Jacob of long ago. To the west lay the vast expanse of the Plain of Esdraelon, known for its rich harvest of barley and wheat. The caravan, however, would swing south into the high foothills of Samaria. When Joseph heard the dragoman had passed the word down that the caravan would cover twenty-three miles and encamp for the night at Dathan, he said goodbye to Mary and the Hannans and for a long time stood watching from the crest at Nazareth.

Time passes quickly with congenial strangers. Talking while walking was like tasting honey on cakes—and one has a tendency to eat too much. The first up-grade was a signal that the climb into the foothills was about to begin. At that point the experienced traveler knew the caravan had gone twelve miles from Nazareth. The dragoman called for a rest stop.

Mary was afraid the disturbance ahead would cause bloodshed, but the Hannans assured her it was only the cameleers shouting and swearing at their camels in order to keep them on their feet. Once a camel went down to his knees to rest, it was very difficult to get him back up while loaded. To unload and reload was a drudgery to be avoided. The affluent merchant's Egyptian cameleers would demand short but frequent stops that aided them in fulfilling their obligations to prayer—and would likewise keep their beasts on their feet.

Although there were two other routes to Jerusalem and the southlands, Jonathan knew that this caravan would take the ridge road, for spring rains had filled the wadis in the lowlands, and many bridges would be washing away. This was the reason for avoiding the route along the Mediterranean shoreline. A third possibility lay east of the Jordan river, which could be worse for the same reasons, plus attacks from men and animals. There wasn't much difference in the distance; it was eighty-seven miles over the winding ridge road.

As Jonathan's little group was finishing a snack of wheat bread and wine, Mary felt someone standing over her. She stopped eating and looked at Jonathan. Their eyes met, and then Jonathan looked up beyond Mary, shouting in surprise: "Tobias! It's good to see you." Jonathan jumped up and embraced the young man.

"Mary," said Deborrah, "this is a dear friend of ours, Tobie. He is a shepherd from Bethlehem."

There was little time for amenities—the caravan was moving—but Tobie, after a brief word with Jonathan, chose to walk beside Mary. He was head and shoulders taller than she; he must have been at least a six-footer, rugged in appearance, his long hair bouncing in the breeze, his face and eyes subdued by a thin growth of beard due to neglect rather than intent. His knee-high cloak looked more like a Roman tunic than a shepherd's robe, drawn tightly around the waist by a plain fabric belt. His bearing and speech belied his youthfulness. Mary thought he was about seventeen.

"Are you from Nazareth?" asked Tobie for an opener.

"Yes, I was born and raised there," she answered.

Tobie then went on to tell that he was employed by an organization that was presently grazing six thousand sheep and that he was in the area in search of more sheep-grazing pastures.

"We have never had more than six sheep," Mary laughed. "But, Mr. Tobie, don't you think you should be walking with the Hannans?"

"Well, maybe, but sometimes I like to do something nice for myself," said Tobie, "—like walk with you?"

"You're the nice one to say that," said Mary, "but, really—I think Jonathan is coming to get you."

"Talk to you later," said Tobie as he slipped back to Jonathan and his three Lycaonian donkeys. Immediately they were in a heated discussion, subdued but tense. Jonathan slapped the carpeting; Tobie kept nodding his head. Because Mary had seen the cargo, she wondered now whether the meeting here were not prearranged and Tobie something more than a shepherd.

The caravan advanced slowly, diagonally along the slope which was leading into the highlands toward Dathan, the city in which Joseph the son of Jacob was sold into slavery by his brothers. "Joseph," thought Mary. "Joseph, my Joseph! I wonder how he is taking my leaving Nazareth. I wonder how long I'll be away? Will I lose my Joseph? I hope Alexander gets the message of my coming to my cousins in Ain Karim. I feel lonely....I shouldn't, for I am two of us."

"Mind if I join Mary?" Tobie addressed Deborrah.

"One must be less inhibited while traveling," responded Deborrah. "Time drags heavily otherwise. Both of your are respectable young people."

Mary was but a short distance ahead, and Tobie, laughing loudly, approached her. "Hey, Mary, do you know how far a camel can travel in a day?"

"Forty miles," said Mary, playing the game.

"Wrong," said Tobie. "It's twenty-five miles. Now the second question—how much weight can it carry?"

"Five hundred pounds." Mary did not have the slightest notion.

"Wrong again," said Tobie. "The average camel will carry a thousand pounds."

"But I thought you were an expert on sheep?"

"Sheep is business. Camels are for fun."

As Tobie came aside Mary, she asked in a subdued voice, "What's in the carpeting on the three donkeys behind us, Tobie? You see, I can ask questions, too."

"Don't tell anyone. It's dried fish." Tobie was obviously on the defensive.

"Wrong," said Mary. "Tell me, where are they being taken?"

"To Herod's palace."

"Wrong again," replied Mary, again playing his game. "But, seriously, Tobie—is there any danger?"

"No, not at all. Will tell you more later. May I ask one more question? What's your destination?'

"Ain Karim, where I'm going to visit a cousin. It's a small community. Do you know where it is?"

"Oh yes, sure! I grazed sheep almost within limits of Jerusalem's most luxuriant suburb. The residents don't like the sheep too close, but grazing laws are on our side. The community looks thinly populated because the estates are large and widespread. Many people walk to and from Jerusalem daily. It's only four miles, more or less, depend on where you live."

"How far is it to Bethlehem?" Mary smiled with interest.

"From Ain Karim?"

"Yes."

"Bethlehem is five miles from Jerusalem, and Ain Karim is about four, which adds up to nine miles—but I'd come for you in a carriage." Tobie had his tongue deep in his cheek.

"Were you born in Bethlehem?"

"Yes, born and raised there."

"Of the tribe of David?"

"No, just the city of David. And you know, I almost was named David, only my father said there were too many Davids, and he named me Tobias. Why do you ask? Does it make any difference?"

"Not really. Did you ever hear of Micah?"

"Micah who? How many sheep does he graze?"

"Tobie...."

"Oh, well, I know he's one of the minor prophets—but—"

Mary felt that she was going too far with the subject and that they would all too soon be talking about the Messiah, her baby, her Chometzla. She asked Tobie to tell her more about Ain Karim.

"They say it's the most beautiful, the most scenic land in all of Palestine—bright white limestone houses dot the landscape along the rivulets that cascade down the fan-like slope into the foamy, jewel-studded Sorek River. The fan is decorated with well-manicured, terraced vineyards and colorful gardens, luscious with verdant foliage and seasonal blooms—"

"Tobie, you sound like you're reading."

"No, but I've heard it a hundred times," said Tobie, "and in all truth I've beheld its beauty often from the surrounding countryside. Your cousin must be rich—how does it feel to be rich?"

"I don't know, Tobie—I'm not rich. My cousins live comfortably, but they are not greedy, and Zachary is a priest, he is dedicated and deeply religious...."

"Sorry, Mary. My sense of humor took a bad twist."

Mary became pensive. Tobie grew a bit restless and soon excused himself and disappeared into the crowd. "Why is Tobie giving me so much attention?" she wondered. "Is he here by God's plan to protect me—and Jesus? He certainly is comfortable—but there is the contraband, sicas in the carpeting, which without a doubt brought him here."

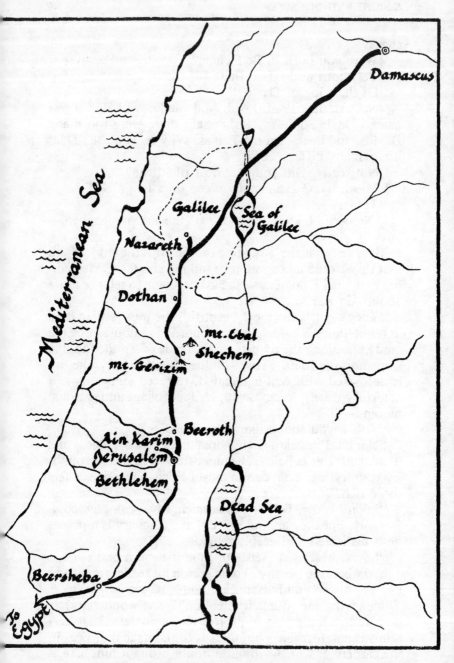

The Caravan Route from the Orient to Egypt.

Chapter 6

The dragoman sent word that the campsite for the night was three miles distant. The sun grew larger as it sank into the jaws of the mountain range, making shadows longer and stirring up chilly wind currents.

Within the hour the caravan reached the historic location, commonly used by the Ridge Road travelers as an overnight rest area. Immediately tents sprang up; the Hannan party quickly took shelter in one of the many caves around the perimeter; tongues of fire appeared here, there, and throughout the area, and people began to prepare for an evening meal. They huddled in small groups, singing and telling stories—stories of laughter and tears, of hope and fears.

A rider on a spirited horse dismounted in front of Hannan's cave, the same weather-beaten face that confronted them when they first joined the caravan that morning.

"I thought there were four of you?" he queried, looking about for Joseph with whom he anticipated having words again.

"There were, Sir," replied Jonathan. "One returned to Nazareth."

Then, looking at Mary, the rider said, "I am the servant

of my master, Emir Zend-Zollo, a wealthy merchant of Alexandria on the Nile. His tent stands the highest in the encampment, as you can see. He sent me to cordially invite you, if you will, to his pavilion in order to discuss a matter of grave importance, the outcome of which may change the course of your whole future life."

The miracle of conception, just seven days ago, had changed her life. Now, another message and another messenger! Mary wondered if this summons related to the first. In an attitude of simple spontaneity, she asked, "Is your name Gabriel?"

"No, my name is Zane. My orders are to escort you to my master. However, if you need to, you can take time to ready yourself."

Mary looked at Deborrah. "I need a little time," she said.

"I shall return shortly," said the rider.

From the shadows of the nearby boulders, Tobie walked out and stood near the fire: "I heard every word he said. I think you ought to see what the old goat wants."

"You had better go with her," said Jonathan.

"Yes, of course, if I am permitted," Tobie glanced at Mary.

Mary smiled a look of confidence at Tobie, and that was it.

"I'm not sure rich-rocks Bend Bollo, or whatever his name, will care to see me. I may be in his way."

"But I need you, Tobie. I fear that this gracious invitation did not originate in heaven."

Jonathan stirred uneasily, aware that he was responsible for Mary. "It will be a great relief to me to know you are with her, Tobie. Thanks."

Mary stood up and turned toward Deborrah. "Do you think I look good enough in these clothes to face the Master of the Pavilion?" She shrugged her shoulders and made a quick turnabout.

"What else?" asked Deborrah. "It's all you have. Don't worry, dear girl, he has already seen your beauty, your person, or he wouldn't be asking you to his tent."

"Thanks for the lift, Deborrah—kind of you to say all that."

"With your kind of beauty, you need not compromise to succeed."

Tobie was told he'd have to wait outside as Mary was escorted by a huge black servant into the recesses of the Zend-Zollo inner sanctum. The plush place looked and smelled like the most exclusive curio shop in Babylon. Myriad lamps of all colors were burning brightly around "His Majesty's throne" and for a moment seemed to vibrate out of focus as Mary curtsied silently.

"I am honored by your coming," declared Emir Zend-Zollo in a deep resonant voice. "You are from Nazareth of Galilee," he continued. "May I ask your name?"

"Mary, the daughter of Joachim, the olive grower." Mary took note of the ponderous hands, every finger was burdened with bands of gold and silver, set with precious gems the size of Papa's ripe olives.

"You are so young," said Zend-Zollo. "Yet, you seem to have complete possession of yourself. What is your destination, might I ask?"

"I am going to Ain Karim," answered Mary softly, "to visit my cousin, a temple priest, Zachary by name." Mary fidgeted with the fabric belt she wore, the recent gift of Joseph.

"This means you have three more days with the caravan, and—uh—two nights ahead of you. You must be aware of the dangers that lie ahead—especially since you are traveling in the unprotected tail of the caravan?" Zend-Zollo's eyes opened round and large under arched eyebrows, beaming at Mary through the framework of a moon face.

"I think he believes he is enticing," thought Mary.

"Please do not feel that I am *forcing* you to accept a life which many a young girl would be glad to have," lied Zend-Zollo clumsily. "I am offering you security and with it many years of complete happiness. All that your eyes can see, and much more, will be yours." He snapped his hands from his wrists in a gesture of dispossession. "Look about you," he advised, surveying the glorious refinements about the room. "This, and a host of servants will be at your beck and call, if you join my household as one of my wives."

"Is this the gateway to fame and power for the Messiah?"

mused Mary. "Is this the Master's plan for me and my baby?

"Speak up, beautiful! Zend-Zollo is not accustomed to waiting."

"Sir, I feel sorry for you," said Mary.

"Why that?" The man was unfamiliar with rejection.

"Your camels reflect your life style, for they carry a burden beyond the limit of a thousand pounds."

"I'm not asking you to be my conscience—weigh your words." A moment of silence passed. Mary stood looking down at the designs on the soft rug under her feet—praying, hoping. "I still desire you to join my household," he continued in a calmer voice. "I will see to it that you are lavishly cared for, and you will enjoy a total security. May I have your consent?"

"Forgive me, Sir, but I have already given consent to another."

"To whom?" demanded Zend-Zollo.

"To one called Gabriel."

"How long ago?"

"Long enough to be with child."

"With child? Hum! I assumed you were a virgin." Zend-Zollo was disappointed indeed.

"I am unworthy of you, your Highness." Her bow was profound. "I beg you dismiss me."

The truth disarmed Zend-Zollo. He squirmed, shifted his weight, then stood up, rang a bell, and demanded that this woman be removed from his presence. Two black, muscular guards lifted Mary by her arms and unceremoniously carried her outside the pavilion. Tobie saw them drop her in the dust. He was quick to run to her side. "What happened? Why this?"asked Tobie.

Mary took off running like a frightened fawn, leaping over rocks shouting in a high-pitched voice:

"Security, he gives security! Like the devil he gives, taking the most! The woman gives her body and soul for a life of security! Elusive security for shameful impurity. A life with white mice for everything nice! What a woman must give for a life of security!"

Mary dropped to the ground with Tobie next to her in the shadows of huge rocks. "What's gone through you,

Mary? You're out of your mind."

Catching her breath, Mary went on as if talking to herself:

"Can a girl enjoy being a man's toy without love? Is it right to be kept and of true love bereft without freedom? Can she play the game—destroy her name—without shame?"

Again Mary sprang to her feet, and began running, Tobie in pursuit. He could hear her half mumbling, half shouting:

"Security, a girl must have love for security! True love to be secure, true love to endure. A man and a baby, a home for a lady. To love and be loved is security, security, security!"

He was finally able to catch her, put his arms around her and bring her to a halt. Her emotions spent, she began to tremble, "I'm cold, Tobie," she said.

"What in Caesar's name happened to you in that pavilion?"

"Do you believe in the devil, Tobie?"

"Yes, of course I do."

"I think I just saw one."

* * * * * * *

It is amazing what the human being can endure when hardship is flavored with challenge and excitement. Inevitably, however, the diminishing of adrenalin and the ongoing routine bring that morning-after feeling of facing reality with what's left. It was the first day away from home for Mary, and that night as she lay wrapped in her sleeping roll near a smoldering fire, she was still tasting the flavor of challenge. The cruel world away from home had not yet caught up with her, but a warning was being sounded by the distant cries of a jackal, howling for its mate. She thought of Zend-Zollo—his act was overplayed, and it made her laugh. But Tobie. In one day's time she had become dependent on him. Was he God-sent? He was certainly nice. "We need him—thank you, God, for Tobie!"

"Mary, are you all right?" asked Deborrah close by. "I thought I heard you talking to someone."

"I'm all right—I guess I was dreaming."

As Mary began her night prayers, she counted likewise the number of days since Gabriel's visit—Jesus was a week old. "And how much older am I? I must be, for I am mothering...conception is over half way. It is beyond the point of no return. A moment equals nine months. How quickly one person becomes two. Let it be done to me." Sleep blanketed her whole body as her thoughts drifted into the crater-like, lavender recesses of her subconsciousness where she found her baby, whole and entire, and with him enfolded by the Holy Spirit, they fell asleep.

Chapter 7

Into the forest of rocks moved the massive caravan led
by the Roman nobleman, Vitellius, slowly and arduously
over ridges, through narrow passages, up and down steep
grades. The dragoman sent word down the line there were
thieves lurking among the rocks and all should take necessary
precautions to secure person and possessions. No one should
pursue a thief, for the cost would be too great, possibly one's
life. Cameleers should be especially careful about temporari-
ly unloaded goods on the high grades, for they would be
stolen before their return.

At midday, the caravan had safely reached the rest area
on the outskirts of Sebaste, the ancient capital of Samaria,
founded by Omri, the father of Ahab. It was Omri's plan
to make Sebaste the capital of all Israel. His enemies had
other plans. Nevertheless, the ambitions of the people kept
the idea alive for centuries paying the heavy price with lives
and much suffering. Stories were told how their early fathers
heroically defended their fortress city against the ponderous
assaults of the Assyrian armies, with the result that Sebaste
was known for its irascible and vicious fighters. The
Judaeans, who constantly downgraded every sector of

Palestine except their own, readily admitted that, although this was a city of worthless jackals, indeed they were fighting jackals.

Two of these fighting jackals were waiting for Jonathan and Tobie and gently greeted them with the kiss of peace, as was their custom. They called one another brothers, for they were joined in a common cause, the restoration of Israel, and were forced to mutual protection by the Romans who hunted them as insurrectionists. Their own people called them Zealots.

Deborrah and Mary were already putting away the utensils they had used for the noonday snack, while the men at a short distance kept busily talking.

"Both of those young men," said Mary, "have an air of good breeding, even though they are shabbily dressed."

"The Judaeans don't like them because they built their own temple on Mt. Gerizim and act independently of Jerusalem, but they have fought to the death to preserve the teachings of Moses. They are brave."

"I think the Romans feel the same, except more so and for different reasons," added Mary, "But the Judaeans don't like the Galileans either."

"Samaria and Galilee have something else in common," continued Deborrah, "—they are both full of Zealots. The Romans, you know, call them Sicarii, because they carry a short dagger, called sica, which they wield with great skill. They say a Sicar can kill without exposing the weapon!"

"Deborrah, are we in trouble?" asked Mary. "I saw the daggers under the carpeting—do you think that—"

"Quiet, here comes Jonathan," Deborrah moved away from Mary.

The caravan moved step by step over rugged terrain. Its destination announced by the dragoman was the biblical city of Shechem, forty-three miles from Nazareth. The thought of being that far from home prompted Mary to call on the good Lord for protection, for herself and all others in the company. Jonathan, the seasoned traveler, assured them that they would have a most enjoyable night of rest in the well-known, ample Shechem caravanserai. "It was built like a fortress," he said. "We'll be there before sunset."

As Jonathan's sure-footed Lycaonian donkeys were passing through a narrow passageway cut around huge boulders, they were unobtrusively relieved of their rolled carpeting. A few boulders later, the carpeting was replaced with similar looking rolls—much lighter, however. It as done so deftly, Jonathan himself hardly noticed the execution of the prearranged plan.

The two young rebels and their cache anxiously sped toward their fortress of granite in the foothills of Mount Ebal, where they commanded a small but ferocious band of Zealots. In time they were destined to become leaders in the National Zealot Council; the one called Judas of Gamala was originally from Galilee, and the other Sadduk, a Pharisee from Samaria. In 6 A.D. they would lead a widespread revolt in the northern provinces in order to disrupt the census which they claimed was being taken mainly for taxing the poor. Their efforts not only ended in failure for themselves, but in time led to the total destruction of Jerusalem in the year 70 A.D. by the Roman legions.

On this day in history, however, Judas and Sadduk rode triumphantly into camp, cheered on by their men who recognized their much-needed cargo. Their impassioned salvos reechoed over cold chasms of inactivity. "This night is for Yahweh," some cried out. "To Sheol with the foreigner!"

After the shouting subsided, Judas the Galilean directed the men to be seated on the ground. "Men," he addressed them, "our weapons are here! Tonight, we raid the garrison of the Roman pigs—after that, we will help ourselves with the spoils of the Vitellius caravan."

"Long live Judas!" they shouted.

"They call you Zealots," continued Judas, "not only because you are giving your best, but because you are giving your all—for the restoration of your fatherland. Tonight Shechem will be free! Tomorrow, Israel! You are preparing for the coming of the Messiah, promised by all the prophets—he will restore the Kingdom. It is your divine privilege to be his coworkers. Tonight belongs to the Messiah!"

Again they cheered—and again.

"Now get this!" cried Judas, demanding attention. "When the moon begins to hide its face behind the crest of Mt. Gerizim, and the enemy sleeps, we will attack. The garrison is first. Only half the soldiers will be there. The other half will be with Vitellius. Our superiority is the new sica. Our advantage is surprise. But above all, Yahweh wills it!"

"Yahweh wills it!" echoed the men and the hills. "Yahweh wills it!"

The rally was not yet finished. Sadduk, who was to lead them, rose to his feet: "Loyal fellow Zealots. I go with you—sica in hand," and he flashed the shining blade beneath his raised left arm, making a savage sound of cutting one's head off. "Kill," he cried. "Cut," he growled. He picked up a soldier close by, raised him off his feet and pretended to cut his head off. The men laughed wildly, drowning out their rising anxiety. "First the outside guards—then inside— then in their beds. Gag and stab every one of the uncircumcised bastards!—Gag and stab! Remember, not one of 'em gets away to warn the caravan."

"Come up now," directed Judas the Galilean, "get your sica. Carve your pet word on its handle, and practice— practice until sundown to use it—with quickness—with one stroke. When the shofar blows, come and get your evening meal; after that there will be absolute silence in camp, and all shall rest until the moon is one hour from Mt. Gerizim."

On the outskirts of the camp, the absolute silence was broken by a guard who shouted "Halt! Who goes there?"

"Tobie and a friend," came the answer.

"State the password," demanded the guard.

"Messiah," said Tobie confidently.

"Pass on," said the guard, putting his hand to his mouth and sending a sharp whistle on to the next guard to signal the all-clear for friendly visitors. As they approached the first campfire, Sadduk greeted Tobie with the kiss of peace. "Sadduk," said Tobie, "this is Mary, the girl from Galilee I told you about, a true friend of the Zealots, dedicated in her own way to the Messiah and the restoration of the kingdom."

"Welcome—to both of you," said Sadduk. "Follow me,

and I will lead you to Judas, your fellow Galilean." He led them to a cave where they found the chief in council with his subordinates.

"Tobie," said Judas coming forward, "we are glad to see you. You arrived at the right moment. You are volunteering to lead the attack inside the caravanserai." Mary looked surprised, but the rest knew the significance of the word *volunteering*. "The drop ladders are hidden here in the southeast corner room on the second story." Tobie leaned over his shoulder to get a better look at the sketch. "When the moon sinks below the Sacred Mountain, you and your men will drop the ladders over the walls at these points, here and here and here. There will be a loud disturbance at the front gate, and at that exact moment our men will scale the walls."

"I follow you, Sir," said Tobie. "Might I suggest that we stampede some of the animals to create further confusion on the inside?"

"Yes," said Judas, "but your primary concern is to get to the gates *and open them*. Don't waste good manpower to stampede within closed gates."

"Yes, Sir."

"Who is this charming young lady?" asked Judas abruptly.

"She came with the sicas," answered Tobie half in jest, but thinking this would please Judas. "She is from Galilee, the land of your birth, Sir. Her name is Mary."

"What part of Galilee are you from, girl?" asked the Chief.

"Nazareth."

"I was born in Cana."

"I've been there—it's beautiful."

"So are you, my dear!" responded Judas, almost out of character.

"Sir," pleaded Mary, "may I speak?"

"Go ahead, but we don't have too much time."

"I asked Tobie to take me along tonight, so that I could speak to you in behalf of the Messiah. He is very near—I know he doesn't approve of what you are doing. Killing is not the answer. Your Messiah will give you a new commandment, 'Love one another'—'Turn the other cheek'—'Forgive your enemies.' That is His kingdom—it is not of this world.''

Tobie began to feel sorry he brought Mary. The chief and his men showed a restlessness that signaled to Mary her time was about up.

''In the name of love—and peace—I offer you my earthly possessions.'' Mary removed Joseph's belt from her waist and set it upon the table in front of Judas the Galilean. ''With this goes the plea that you restrain yourselves from killing and plundering, that you practice love in place of hate, and that you believe in the presence of the Messiah. All things are possible with him.''

Mary stepped back and was supported by the strong arm of Tobie. A hush fell over the assembly. Wheels of conscience ground audibly Mary's words into a fine grist.

''We must reject your feminine niceties,'' said Judas, ''with regrets. The Roman does not play the game you describe, so neither can we. We must hasten the coming of the Messiah by eliminating the oppressor.''

''But Sir, love begets love!'' pleaded Mary. ''He who lives by the sica will—''

Getting the sign from Sadduk, Tobie took Mary by the hand, saying, ''Let's go, Mary.''

''Tobie, you believe me, don't you? Strength lies in the Spirit, not in armor—Yahweh is not second to Caesar—''

''Don't put Yahweh to the test, Mary. Remember, Moses never did see the Promised Land, nor did Jacob erect any great monument except a polluted well a stone's throw from here.''

Mary brushed a tear from her cheek. Somehow her feminine promptings spilled over, in spite of her great desire to show herself strong before these mountain men. At the entrance standing guard was a boy.

''Aren't you from Nazareth?'' she asked, noting the boy's Galilean nose and dark eyes.

''Yes,'' replied the guard.

''Is your father's name Simon?''

''Right!'' he replied. ''And my name is Simon ben Simon. I'm now a member of the Zealot Party.'' He stood tall and looked proud.

Mary felt a power pass through her. "From Chometzla," she thought. Was it a compensatory effect after the frustration of meeting the fighting men inside the cave? Later on in her life, she would meet Simon again, and he would be called "Simon the Zealot," even though he would then be pursuing a course of peace and love for the Kingdom.

Chapter 8

The caravanserai at Shechem loomed large in the luscious valley hanging like a hammock between Mt. Gerizim and Mt. Ebal. It was a popular stopping place, for it served travelers off the North-South Ridge Road and the East-West Trail from the Jordan River Ghor to the Mediterranean. Tonight it would be occupied only by the caravan coming from the north with its precious cargo and distinguished persons.

Slowly and with ponderous dignity, animals and things and people were swallowed up by the huge gates which opened to a spacious quadrangle surrounded by a two-story building twenty feet high. On the ground floor were open stalls, while the second floor was lined with many small doors to many small rooms. After all had entered, they looked back and saw the only entrance barred by massive wooden beams placed horizontally in thick iron brackets.

Vitellius, sporting a Roman background, was wont to refer to the cubicles on the second floor as Maccabean torture chambers. He had his men set up his pavilion near the entrance. That left the center of the courtyard for the rich merchant Zend-Zollo, which suited him just fine. Jonathan's group, the am-ha-arez, found space near the rear in one of the animal stalls, where he could keep an eye on his donkeys.

The secure environment brought on a relaxation that in turn prompted an air of festivity. Physical tiredness undermines discipline and gives rise to natural instincts. Camp fires blazed; there was plenty of food; they sang and danced, and then the dragoman announced from the balcony, "The day is done, and the night's rest begins—Whatever else must be, let it be done in silence. The caravan departs one hour before sunrise."

Later in the night a young couple who identified themselves as Tobie and Mary, members of the caravan, gained admission into the tightly-secured caravanserai. They noticed lights were on in both pavilions. Animals were stirring reflectively in their stalls. They could hear them breathing as they walked by. A bright moon shone over the turret in the direction of Mt. Gerizim. Its silvery light burnished all things with a cool, metallic reflection that bordered on artificiality, the kind one sees on a stage of the Greek theater in Athens.

After separating from Tobie, Mary attempted to find sleep in the room she shared with two other women on the loggia. As she recited the Shemoneh Esreh, her thoughts drifted to the camp of the Zealots. "I guess I made a fool of myself —but I had to do it.... Love *is* better than hate.... Peace is better than war. Hope I never have to tell Joseph what I did with his belt and money. But maybe that would be easier to explain than Tobie—Oh, Jesus, why is Tobie here? Why is he so likable?... Is he human? How can I repay his devotion, his care for *us*? How must I love him?" She hastened to thank God for Tobie and all that happened this day. "But God," she prayed, "can you stop the massacre tonight—?" She stiffened with fright when suddenly the room turned dark. "The moon has dropped behind the peak of Mt. Gerizim." She continued her prayer.

Her hopes were shattered when the death cry of a wounded soldier pierced the stillness of the night at the gate. Guards hurried to open the gate and let him in. He was slumped over his horse, blood flowing profusely from his mouth. "The garrison has fallen! Zealots are coming!"

Many of the onlookers were hanging over the railing of the loggia where Mary saw Tobie and a handful of men running toward the far corner with drop-ladders. It was early, she thought, but the arrival of the wounded soldier alarmed them. Tobie's ladder hardly hit the ground when up came a Zealot saying, "That bloody soldier was stabbed three times by myself—How in hellfire did he get here alive?" Two more Zealots came up the ladder.

"Sadduk!" exclaimed Tobie, recognizing his leader. "How about the garrison?"

"It's secured. All those uncircumcised Roman pigs have been left bleeding."

"Look! They've just secured the gate," said Tobie.

"The three of you jump from the north side," directed Sadduk pointing to Tobie and two others. "We three will take it from the south—Those gates must be opened, even if it kills every last one of us!"

Everyone in the caravanserai seemed to be running into the square, along with the frenzied animals. The dragoman kept shouting, "Everyone stay in your rooms!" Then came the thunderous sounds of shouting men and pounding hoofs from beyond the walls. Sadduk gave the order to jump, and six brave men as one leaped in front of the gates, lifted the barriers, and in poured the raging Zealots swinging their sicas—right, then left—and galloping into the crowd. Deborrah and Mary saw Jonathan whipping the animals out of their stalls, camels heavily laden, and horses, and cattle, stumbling and bumping one another; some fell to the ground and never got up, both men and beasts. Women screamed as they pushed and ran up the stairways to the safer level of the loggia. Mary covered her face with her hands as the pavilion of Zend-Zollo like a mantle turned white with heat, burst into flame, and dropped down upon the master, his jewels, his women, and his servants.

The Zealots funneled back through the gates along with the camels upon which had been tied the spoils of war by their insiders. There were also the things each soldier could snatch himself and the sheep and goats they had in flight. But the dead and the living and the wounded knew that only the gods of war could be the victors. Only theirs was the

hour of placation in which human sacrifice was offered and
many maimed for life. The shamefaced moon of lunatics,
lovers, and warriors now lay hidden behind the sacred mountain, enveloping in darkness the feelings of guilt and sorrow.

Just as other women searched for their men, so Mary and
Deborrah now went in search of Tobie and Jonathan. When
they came to the guard house at the gate, Mary asked, "Have
you taken any prisoners?"

"Yeah, they're in the next cell."

They weren't allowed to enter, but Deborrah looked
through the doorway and let out a scream of horror that
left her rigid as stone. She saw Jonathan sitting in the dirt,
his head against the wall a bloody mess. He was chained,
both wrists and ankles. Deborrah again attempted to enter,
but was restrained and ordered to leave. Mary took a second look into the prison cell—but Tobie wasn't there. She
caught up with Deborrah and put her arm around her.

* * * * * * *

At daybreak, a new dragoman shouted orders for the
decimated caravan to form in preparation for leaving
Shechem. Vitellius sat dejected in his charred chariot surrounded by a dozen Roman soldiers into whose custody the
prisoners were placed. Vitellius was perplexed as to how he
could dispose of the prisoners, for they were a liability to
him traveling through Samaria and Judaea, bating onlookers
along the open country. Likewise, there was the constant
threat that so long as he had the prisoners, their brother
Zealots would return to reclaim them. After a quick con-
sultation with his aides, he dispatched a messenger to King
Herod.

Zend-Zollo not only lost his life, but most of his possessions. Only a pitiful semblance of his splendor rode on a
camel bearing two of his wives, followed by a half dozen
servants carrying bundles. The am-ha-arez fared best of all,
for they weren't important enough for the gods of war to
consume.

"Deborrah," said Mary, "let us thank God we were
spared."

"How can I?" lamented Deborrah. "I would rather be

dead with my husband.''

"God knows best when life begins and when it ends for all of us,'' Mary attempted to console her companion. "Look at this crate,'' she continued. "All the pigeons have flown.''

"Do you think they've gone to Ain Karim?'' asked Deborrah.

"Alexander could have, but the other two know only to return to Nazareth, and I'm sure all three went together.'' Mary's face became drawn like ancient parchment as she visualized Papa checking the birds for messages which wouldn't be there. He would know that the only message was the unwritten one, the one that told him Mary had had an accident, and the pigeons had been released from a broken crate.

Chapter 9

"**It's not a nice day for traveling,**" said Joachim look-ing out the kitchen window. "The wind is blowing hard from the west, and rain clouds are heavy as far as the eye can see. Mar-ree and the Hannans must be preparing at this mo-ment to leave the comfort of the Shechem caravanserai."

"Day after tomorrow Alexander should be flying in from Ain Karim to tell us of their safe arrival." But Anna spoke with an air of fear.

"Which reminds me," interjected Joachim, "I should feed the pigeons before it starts raining."

Left alone, Anna began to hum her familiar, sacred chants, and because Mary was bearing heavily on her heart, she drifted into the longing lyric of the Song of Solomon:

"[She has] love no flood can quench, no torrents drown.
Were a man to offer [her] all the wealth of his house,
to buy love,
contempt is all he would purchase!
Our sister is little, her breasts are not yet formed.
What shall we do for our sister
on the day she is spoken for?" (Sg. 8:7)

Little did Anna realize that when she sang like this with

the family, and sometimes joined by them, she was teaching
Mary a moral principle that would stand by her in times
of stress. But Anna worried about Joseph. He had certain
rights over her daughter, but now she was gone, and her
return was uncertain. Would she have to prompt Joachim
to confront Joseph about this? To tell him all? It would be
the fair thing to do. "I wonder what our cousin, Priest
Zachary, will advise Mary."

"No message? God have mercy! How about the other
two?"

"They're back—no message!" Joachim sat down on his
cot. Alexander walked softly on his lap. "Speak, Alexander!
Tell us what happened!"

"Yahweh, Sabbaoth," prayed Anna audibly, "listen, God
of Jacob, God our shield, be kind to your anointed one,
Mary, our daughter, your favored one!" She scurried about
the house as if she were trying to find something she had
lost—something of her innermost being.

"What did I do with her? Where is my little girl?" She
hurried into the garden, back through the house, into the
storeroom, looked on the mantle, on the table. She ran to
Mary's room. There she stood before the empty bed, crying, "Dear God, did we do wrong to send her out there,
so far from home?" She wiped the tears from her face and
slowly now returned to Joachim lying on his cot. "I have
a feeling," she said "that our little one is dead, death is here,
it has come—*Joachim!*" she cried. "Joachim, my husband,
my dear one!" Anna dropped to her knees.

Joachim lay trembling, his head back, eyes wide open,
mouth agape. Alexander was cowering under his amiable
master's chin as though he would prop it up, but in vain.

"Joachim, look at me!" cried Anna. "What's happened?" She began to rub his marble-like hands, then she
encircled him, attempting to stop his trembling. Her face
touched his; he was motionless and cold. She struggled to
make him warm.

"Anna," he haltingly said, "It is finished with me. I have
failed. Mar-ree...Mar-ree...."

"Be quiet, Joachim, I'll fetch you a hot drink."

"Lord," he said, "let me be her sacrifice....Spare

her....I die that she may live...."

Anna dropped her head and prayed. Then, she looked up directly into Alexander's eyes. He kept bobbing his head.

"Alexander," she said, "Alexander, this minute you're going to fly to Ain Karim."

Chapter 10

Vitellius stirred restlessly in his makeshift tent. He turned to his aides and said, "It would be better to judge and execute the prisoners of Shechem today. We've already made heroes out of rebels by waiting."

The carvan, or rather what was left of it, had halted near the sacred, ancient city of Lebonah. Nearby were the heights of Shiloh where the ark of the covenant was kept, a national shrine in honor of Judaic Law.

"Sir, you have a most fitting temple of justice in which to hold court," offered Flavius with a grin. "The ten Commandments of the Ark are inscribed in the hearts of all Israelites."

"Must we bring rain to a flooded area?" asked Claudius Vera, one of Vitellius' more learned aides.

"Someone's at the door," declared Flavius.

"Let him in," said Vitellius.

"By your leave," said the stranger, "I bring you greetings from my Master Herod, His Majesty, the King of Judaea."

"Very well," responded Vitellius. "Speak your message."

"Sir, it is here, bound by the royal seal." The messenger handed him the scroll. Vitellius, suspecting this would be

a proclamation giving him the authority he sought, asked
Claudius Vera to read it.

> *Your Eminence, Vitellius, honorable Emissary
> from Rome, His Majesty King Herod herewith
> delegates you to act as Supreme Judge in the trial
> of the "Shechem Six" in a place of your designa-
> tion. After sentence is passed, the prisoners shall
> be placed in the custody of the Senior Officer of
> your company, who will carry out the execution.*

"Sir, if I may make an observation," said Claudius Vera,
"the decretum from Herod obviously prejudges the rebels.
It even suggests 'execution'."

"This should be a short trial, Sir," quipped Flavius. "Our
soldier-scholar Vera would introduce delaying complexities."

"In the trial for the death penalty, you alone cannot act
as judge," continued Vera. "The law requires three judges."

"The king has designated me," said Vitellius, "as
'Supreme Judge.' I am interested in justice." But the young
Roman didn't sound too eager.

"Burn it all, Sir," insisted Flavius. "This must be done
quickly. We have no men to guard the Temple. Either we
kill them, or they kill us." Vitellius continued, "Let the of-
ficers of the court be appointed—and the courtroom
prepared."

"Where?" asked Flavius.

"Any ideas?"

"The sacred Hall of the Ark of Shiloh!" said Flavius with
a diabolical grin, raising his eyebrows. "All should know
that the laws of the sovereign Roman Empire have super-
seded the ancient decalogue of Moses once enshrined there."

"Only you would think of such blasphemy—Let it be
done." Vitellius dismissed his aides: "Be ready at two
o'clock this afternoon."

* * * * * * *

Up the steep and sinuous road that led from Lebonah to
the heights of Shiloh, Mary and Deborrah followed closely
upon the heels of Jonathan and the other five prisoners,
chained and heavily guarded. When they reached the Hall,
the simple folk, the am-ha-arez from the caravan and the

countryside had already gathered, ready to participate in the trial. Roman law permitted an open forum. Some anticipated their chances by renaming the Hall of the Decalogue "The Hall of the Monologue." Only the sentence of death would be spoken, as prearranged.

Inside, Vitellius, only recently come of age as a Roman citizen, banged the gavel and loudly proclaimed, "This court is now in session. Will the clerk read the official document establishing jurisdiction!"

"Vitellius, eminent Citizen of Rome, present emissary of Augustus, the Emperor, in the Province of Palestine, is hereby commissioned to act as sole Judge in the trial of the six prisoners apprehended in the insurrection at Shechem, signed Herod, King of Palestine."

"Set forth the prisoners, and let us hear the accusations," directed the honorable Vitellius.

There was an ominous clanging of chains as the bloodied, bandaged men lined up against the wall facing the bench.

"The State wishes to identify these men, Your Honor," said the prosecutor. "Would the clerk call the names?"

"Nehemiah, farmer, citizen of Samaria!

"Ezra, shepherd, citizen of Bethlehem!" Mary startled when she heard "Bethlehem" and quickly looked up, but it wasn't Tobie.

"Hezekiah, maker of pottery, citizen of Cana.

"Jonathan ben Hannan, silversmith, citizen of Nazareth." Deborrah broke out with a shrieking cry that found sympathetic wailing throughout the assembly. For a long moment the trial was held up, as Vitellius banged away demanding, "Order!"

"Malachi, Pharisee," continued the clerk. "Your honor, we know no more about this prisoner."

"Are you sure he is not a Roman citizen?" asked the judge.

"Sure."

"Are any of the others?" If they were not, then Vitellius could continue his plan for a short trial and impose Herod's pre-judgments. Only Romans had rights and privileges which if not respected would get Vitellius in trouble with his people back home in the higher courts.

"There are none, Your Honor."

"Now on with the accusation," ordered Vitellius.

"The State calls the centurion of the Shechem garrison," stated the prosecutor. After identifying himself as Gaius Sempronius, the centurion declared that he was with Vitellius in his pavilion at the Caravanserai making his report when all hell broke loose. "I dashed from the pavilion," he said, "and saw three men leap to the ground from the loggia. Assisted by others, they opened the gates. The one with his arm in the sling, and another with bandaged head stand there," he pointed. "The third one got away apparently, for I don't see him here. I struck both of these men to the ground, but only after it was too late and the Zealots came riding in."

"There are four other prisoners here," remarked Vitellius. "Did you see any one of them during the raid?"

"I saw that one, I believe he was identified by the clerk as the silversmith from Galilee."

"What was he doing when you saw him?"

"I mustered a group to put out fires, and as we went by the animal stalls, I saw him whipping and releasing the animals into the stampede. I struck him down and turned him over to one of the guards."

"What about the others?"

"Didn't see them."

"Your Honor," said the prosecutor, "the state charges these three men with willful and deliberate participation in insurrection against the government of Shechem. They are Nehemiah, Hezekiah, and Jonathan ben Hannan."

"At this time," said Vitellius, "I direct that you continue with the witnesses."

"The State presents another eyewitness, Antonius Varus, who although wounded rode bravely to the caravanserai to warn of the attack of the Zealots." Antonius Varus was carried into the witness chair. His appearance caused a reaction from the crowd, for they had thought he was dead. After order was restored, Antonius told his story, how he was standing guard at the Mt. Gerizim gate of the garrison, when suddenly two of his buddies standing guard with him dropped to the ground, their throats slit back to the spine, bleeding. In the moment he gained, he withstood the attacker, but was overpowered and fell wounded. He recovered and rode on to the caravanserai.

Among other accusers, one was Emir Zend-Zollo's rider, Zane, who swore that he knew that Jonathan ben Hannan and his friend, Tobie by name, transported weapons to the Zealots. Upon being questioned, he admitted that he did not see any transferral of the weapons take place, and that there were always three loaded Lyconian donkeys. What he saw at the caravanserai the night of the attack was the same as the others saw.

It was the duty of the Judex in the Roman Law to act as jury and to pronounce guilt or non-guilt. At least this was the one item in which Vitellius was deeply interested, so he could expedite the trial. "This court pronounces the accused guilty as accused. The penalty for insurrection and murder is death by crucifixion. I hereby appoint Gaius Sempronius, centurion, as magistrate, to carry out the sentence."

"I have understood your order, Sir, and will carry it out."

"This court is now—" Vitellius was startled.

"Your Honor, your laws permit an open forum before sentence is pronounced. This has been slighted." It was the voice of a young girl, nervously high, but calmly correct.

"We never spoke to the contrary," replied Vitellius. "Do you wish to be heard? If so, identify yourself and speak!"

"My name is Mary. I am the daughter of Joachim, the olive grower in Nazareth, Galilee. I question the severity of the penalty you have imposed. First of all, because we have heard only one side—that is the accusation, and the prosecutor did not ask for any defense." Mary came closer to the bench as she continued to talk and kept looking directly into the face of the judge, who didn't seem to be too much older than she was.

"Sir," interjected the prosecutor, "magnanimity will not substitute for competence. This is post factum. The case has already been decided."

"Let her speak." said Vitellius with feigned confidence.

"Thank you, Your Honor. Expediency prevailed over justice in this trial," continued Mary. "Rash judgment is not a deterrent to crime. It rather arouses the conscientious to commit further crime. The prisoners are not all equally guilty, and yet all received equal penalty. Theirs was the inalienable right to self defense, a choice between slavery and freedom. They chose freedom as any human being would. The fact that they chose violence to gain freedom only emphasizes the fact that their slavery was unbearable."

"Do you have specifics, young lady?" asked Vitellius.

"King Herod's crimes have become household words. He is spoken of as a usurper to the throne, as a foreigner, and as one conspiring with the Romans to destroy Israel from within. My witnesses, Sir, are the poor of the country."

"We shall not have the king maligned in this court, young lady," declared Vitellius sternly.

"Your appointment to this court comes from a highly questionable source," continued Mary.

"This trial was terminated once," interjected the prosecutor. "I see no need to continue this useless process."

"Do you have anything more to say?" asked Vitellius, showing more interest in the girl than the subject matter.

"Yes, thank you, Sir. The trial of the silversmith from Galilee, Ben Hannan, should have been held independently of the others. He was accused of releasing animals, and not of murder and insurrection. Nothing more was proven."

"Very well. Let Jonathan ben Hannan step forward," announced Vitellius.

"He is unable to walk, Sir," said the prosecutor.

"I hereby mitigate your sentence to flogging, and let it be noted that the flogging shall end at thirty-nine lashes."

"Sir, he will not survive it," she said.

"We will have order in this court!" said Vitellius. "Young lady, you have had your say, now I ask you to remain silent."

Members of the court, as well as the people assembled, began to stir restlessly. It looked like a private dialogue was growing in intensity between two persons. Mary wouldn't be denied as long as she felt that Vitellius didn't mean what he said. Vitellius returned to her. He thought he was gaining a promising relationship. Just as he faced her, Mary said, "Sir, your laws declare that the judge shall not take on an accusing attitude toward the accused, as you have. If the judge speaks at all, it is written, he shall speak 'in behalf of the accused.' '' The crowd stirred, there was loud talking and shuffling, and it moved toward the bench.

"Order!" cried Vitellius. "We must have order in the court!" Then again addressing Mary: "Young lady, restrict your words to the prisoners. It is not I who am on trial."

"Is the judge greater than the law?" Mary spoke softly, not wanting to enrage the crowd. Rather she aimed at pleasing Vitellius.

"The accusations have been clearly made and established," declared His Honor. Ignoring Mary and rising to his feet, he rapped the gavel as loudly as he could and announced, "This court is dismissed!"

Within minutes, the Honorable Vitellius was in his decrepit tent, stomping and kicking up the dirt, and unmercifully castigating himself: "Garbage—just plain garbage—I'm not a judge. Cursed be that Idumaean slave Herod who tricked me into thinking that I was!"

"Everyone knows these condemned men are Zealots," consoled Claudius Vera, "and they are killed on sight. You, Sir, at least gave them a hearing."

"Imagine that slip of a girl from Galilee, pleading what Romans term 'insurrection.' She has the gall to say it is 'self-defense'," fumed Vitellius.

"Notice, too, how she detected your expediency to be a cheap substitute for justice," added Claudius Vera. "I thought you'd pop your eyes out."

"I would rather have served justice."

"Shall we blame King Herod?"

"We're sure to see more of him." Vitellius was dejected. "But Mary? Who said 'nothing good comes from Galilee'? She bothered me—but pleasantly. She stood there saying, 'Rash judgment is not a deterrent to crime'." He raised his voice and his arms. " 'The judge shall speak in behalf of the accused.' You know, Claudius, I'd truly like to hear more from her. I hate to admit it."

"Perhaps the gods will favor you, Sir," said Claudius Vera. "Isn't it strange how history moves mankind into contradiction? The Jews came one day to General Pompey in Damascus begging him to bring stability to their nation. He did. He eliminated Alexander Jannaeus and his cruel crucifixions of his own people—eight hundred at one time—and brought a period of peace. And now the Jews would kill us."

"You've been reading again, soldier," jibed Flavius.

"I'm surprised you recognize the action of the intellect," responded Claudius Vera. "You haven't read six inches of scroll in the past dozen years."

"Go on, Claudius, tell us some more," urged Vitellius.

"Well, it was five years before the Jews came to Pompey," continued Claudius with delight, "that Alexandra, wife of Jannaeus, rotten to the core, died and left the country up for grabs. Her two sons, Hyrcanus II and Aristobulus II, and Antipater the Idumaean, fought for supremacy until the hills of the land looked like forests of crosses with human blood so deep it caused rivulets to flow into the valleys—"

"I don't believe it," interrupted Flavius. "That's too much."

"Pompey found no one with whom he could negotiate." Claudius Vera ignored his friend. "Too many leaders and not enough followers create a vacuum of authority."

"How true," mused Vitellius.

"Pompey went so far as to enter into the very inner sanctum of the Temple, which the Jews considered the source of all authority, and to his dismay he found nothing."

"This may not have been the fault of the Jews," commented Vitellius.

"But it was," insisted Claudius Vera. "Tacitus, our renowned historian, wrote *'vacuum sedem, et inania arcana,'* meaning, in summary, 'there is nothing everywhere'."

Things were getting too pedantic for Flavius; he jumped up. "How long are you two going to carry on while the Shechem Six cry for vengeance?"

"You're right, Flavius," agreed Vitellius. "Give the order to break camp. Off we go to Jerusalem!" He then turned to Claudius Vera. "Would you consider it advisable for me to take the girl from Galilee along with us? I was thinking—"

"By no means, Sir," replied Claudius Vera. "It would jeopardize our safe arrival at Herod's Palace. The Zealots would pursue us into Sheol, and Herod would not consider us welcome. It is out of the question."

"Herod should talk about proprieties. Nevertheless, thanks, Claudius. How far is it to Bethel?" asked Vitellius.

"Thirteen miles, Sir"

"We should be there after sunset. Leave the tent as it is, and light a lamp or two. After the populace buries its dead, it'll come this way for trouble. We'll gain time if they think we are still here. Take nothing more than one horse for each man."

* * * * * * *

Early the next morning before sunrise, Mary and Deborrah left Lebonah, where they had found shelter for the night, and started up the narrow, winding pathway that led to the heights of Shiloh. They had been instructed to return to claim their wounded and flogged man. Mary's pleading had begotten hope for Deborrah, but within her heart she felt the chance for Jonathan's survival was minimal, just as it was for her country. The trial was but another small nail driven into the body politic, Israel, that would hold it crucified forever. History recorded their final breath of opposition to the Romans in the year 70 A.D. when not a stone was left upon stone of the Temple at Jerusalem. Only the Messiah, the Son of God, present at this trial as an amion, the little lamb, in the mother's womb, would live to say, "My Kingdom is not of this world," and then himself be crucified as "the Lamb of God who takes away the sins of the world" (Jn. 18:36; Jn. 1:29).

Half way up the mountainside, the two sorrowful women halted before five crosses bearing the remains of withered human beings draped over wood like vines cut from their branches. The Romans chose this stage-like plateau overlooking the serpentine road from Lebonah to Jerusalem, where passersby could study the current political penalties of insurrection. Five of the Shechem Six were dead.

Flogging was introduced into Palestine by the Romans as a punishment for crimes covered by Roman law. The Jews adopted it in time with a few ameliorations, such as a less cruel whip and a limited number of lashes. They didn't need

to borrow cruelty from others; they had themselves devised
ingenious ways to deal with criminals: burning in a dung
pile, stoning, beheading, and strangling. Flogging, for the
Jews, was an added punishment to crucifixion. In Jonathan
ben Hannan's case, it was a substitution and an ameliora-
tion. For Mary's unborn Son, it would be imposed before
crucifixion. Historians have said crucifixion was introduced
into Palestine by the Phoenicians and reached an all-time
sadistic height with Alexander Jannaeus, who ordered eight
hundred prisoners crucified before a captive audience of their
wives and children, who in turn were slaughtered on the
scene before the crucified died. As a postscript, but none-
theless important, the chronicles add, "while Jannaeus
himself banqueted with his concubines."

Mary and Deborrah reached the summit that was Shiloh
and joined a few am-ha-arez already there, warming
themselves on the sunny side of the Hall of the Covenant.
A tall, robust Roman soldier approached. "Where can I find
the wife of Jonathan ben Hannan?" he asked the crowd.

"This is his wife," answered Mary, putting her arm
around Deborrah.

"Madam." The soldier was compassionate. "I am instructed to inform you that your husband passed away during the night. His death was caused by the severity of the
wounds inflicted in the uprising at Shechem. Sorry."

Once again, Deborrah wailed and swooned. Mary and
others sought to console her. Mary heard the departing
soldier say, *"One more carcass, one more grave, how many
more does mother earth crave?"*

* * * * * * *

The sun had crossed the meridian when the caravan started
to move southward. What a ghastly sight it was, waggling
along like a severed serpent's tail, sometimes disordered and
coiled, sometimes elongated. Its collective remnant mass,
mostly on foot, was pitiably led by a bedraggled dragoman,
long haired and bearded, an outcast from Cana of Galilee.
Next to him walked Mary, leading the Hannan donkey with
Deborrah riding dejected and incommunicado. The
dragoman admitted to Mary that this was his first experience

in leading a caravan, if one could call it that, but no one seemed to harbor any misgivings about their safety. Poverty and misery rode together unchallenged, having no other cargo in their possession. "Next stop Beeroth!" cried the dragoman.

* * * * * * *

Deborrah startled when she suddenly heard Mary's cry, "Tobie! How wonderful to see you!" Tobie stood at the entrance of the Beeroth caravanserai with his arms opened wide to embrace Mary and Deborrah. "Tobie!" exclaimed Mary. "You've come from heaven."

"From Sheol!" snapped Tobie. "But welcome to Beeroth," he said bowing in an exaggerated manner. "Miladies," he continued, "your chambers await your gracious presence."

The shepherd from Bethlehem was growing in dignity and stature, and with the spoils of war given him by the Zealots, he had provided separate adjacent rooms for his guests.

"What a lovely Babylonian rug," noticed Mary as she stepped into her small but clean room. "And I detect a scent of spring in the air—oh, there it is, a spray of anemone— my favorite flowers...and look at the freshly cut olive branches. Oh, Tobie, it all reminds me of home. How good of you to do it. But it reminds me of Papa. Is he all right? And think of all the yard work Mama's having to do."

"Have a chair, Mary," Tobie invited them to two small chairs and a table against the wall. "I see my desire to make the room homelike boomeranged. It made you worry about home."

"You shouldn't have done all this—just for one night's lodging." She was smiling again.

"You deserve much more, Mary. I can't explain it but whenever I'm with you, I feel like I'm in the presence of a true lady, a somebody wonderful. Never had this feeling ever before.

"You're the superhuman, Tobie. You must be an angel. Did you ever hear of Gabriel?"

"Who?"

"God's messenger, Gabriel."

"Never did."

"I was beginning to think you were Gabriel."

They both laughed, and Tobie asked, "Say, didn't you ask Zane, Zend-Zollo's horseman, the same question?"

"I did, come to think of it."

"It doesn't flatter me any."

"Poor Zend-Zollo," said Mary, "how like a fable is the security of man. What he offered me, he no longer has for himself."

"And yet this is all we strive for," remarked Tobie.

"All? I'm surprised. You don't impress me as a man whose ambitions are centered around money and possessions."

"Not really, 'all' I guess. But what else is there? Search for power, if not for wealth?"

"Try again."

"Happiness?"

"You're closer."

"Security. Security that is unbroken, in riches and in poverty, in life and in death—that's it, isn't it?"

"Its a form of security, but I like to call is "peace in doing God's will'."

"That makes it remote—out of reach—intangible. God's will? What's that? How do I know it?"

"It's what you think it is," answered Mary, "after you've thought it out."

"That could be anything you want it to be," persisted Tobie.

"The test is," continued Mary, "that you are at death what you wanted to be in life—mature."

"You make it sound so easy."

"Tobie, I was afraid I'd never see you alive after Shechem. I hear you jumped a camel in the stampede and rode to safety."

"Right, I hung on like a coward all the way. The order was, 'First ones in, first ones out!' We took the spoils to Mt. Ebal." Tobie stood up and walked over to the small window, looking out. "Mary, was the fear of never seeing me again prompted by the thought of losing me, or just the fear of death?" Her answer would mean everything to him.

He was taking the risk.

"How can I lose something I don't have, Tobie? It's a fine distinction you make. I don't want to mislead you."

"Putting it plainly," said Tobie, "I wondered whether you wanted me alive because you love me?"

"You are a lovable person, and many a girl could love you. But for me, it is out of the question."

"You leave me without hope."

"Emir Zend-Zollo had me carried out of his pavilion when he heard the truth. I'm afraid of what you might do if I tell you."

"Try me," challenged Tobie.

"I don't know where to begin," said Mary. "Perhaps with Gabriel? Only this time, I'm dead serious. This messenger of God came to me a few days ago and told me I was to be the mother of a child, and told me his name shall be Jesus, the Messiah. It frightened me—"

"Only a few days ago?" asked Tobie. "In Nazareth?"

"I count the days: exactly eleven," said Mary. "I asked Gabriel how this could happen, since I was not married— solemnly engaged, yes, but not living as a wife. He told me not to worry, that the Holy Spirit would come over me and I would be with child."

There was a pause. Tobie asked, "Anything more?"

"Gabriel vanished, and I felt I was alone—well not quite alone, for strange things were happening inside of me."

"Are you with child now?" His voice low, as if walking on tip-toe.

"Yes."

"How would you know? It's only eleven days."

"It's not only that I believe Gabriel, but I know it. I have lived it every hour, every minute since it happened."

"Could it be just imagination? I mean just a dream? So many girls are making this claim nowadays."

"I don't blame you for saying that, Tobie. I'm a total stranger to you. Why should you believe me?"

"But, you know, you're different. I kind of want to believe you."

"Thanks."

Tobie began to grind out some male logic in the silence

that ensued. This girl is pregnant, not married. Shouldn't she be married to protect herself and child? People will not understand. There could be serious trouble for her. She's sweet, brave, sensible. "Mary," he began aloud, "you need a husband—and—and I am willing to be that man in your life."

Tears appeared on her apple cheeks. She wiped them off as she searched for words. "Tobie, you could have stoned me, but you didn't. You could have laughed at me, but you didn't. Back home, there is Joseph to whom I am solemnly engaged. He has already settled the dowry, made the gifts, and has a place for us to live. You know what all this means according to our Law?"

"Yes, every Jew knows. And I now could be stoned with you if they found us alone in this room."

"How easily could we be misjudged."

Tobie looked apprehensively toward the entrance. All was quiet. "You perform no miracles to help me believe, Mary, except you yourself. You are a beautiful person."

"Now I have three who believe—my mother, my father, and you—only a few billion more to go!" Mary sighed audibly in relief.

"Three?" questioned Tobie. "How about Joseph?"

"He doesn't know."

"How in the world will he take it when he finds out?" Tobie sensed a ray of hope. "If anything happens to Joseph, or if he fails you, promise me you'll come to me."

"I don't expect to have all the answers," she said. "I only keep myself ready to do what God wants me to do. I wait for Him."

"I'll wait, too," said Tobie graciously. "However, up until now, I've been tagging after you with an occasional notion that I might be able to take you home with me to Bethlehem."

"And at times I wondered whether God was trying to tell me something." Mary was pensive. "I am fully aware of what he said through the mouths of his prophets—that Jesus shall be born in Bethlehem, the city of David."

"You see," said Tobie, "I have the prophets on my side."

Then there was a knock on the door. Tobie and Mary

both stood up. Reality rattled reverie. "Who's there?" she asked.

"May I come in?" pleaded a weak, quivering voice. "My sorrow is unbearable. I am alone!"

"Oh, it's Deborrah," sighed Mary in relief. "Please come in. Forgive me for leaving you alone for so long, but Tobie and I lost all sense of time."

"Have my chair, Deborrah," said Tobie, helping her to sit. Mary immediately poured fresh water into a cup provided by Tobie and mixed it with wine drawn from a decanter which she carried in her bag. The fermented juice of the grape was safer to drink than most water in strange places. No one traveled without it. Tobie sat down on the Babylonian rug and crossed his legs under him.

"Thanks for the lovely room," said Deborrah. "I wish Jonathan were here to share it. Do you miss him, too, Tobie?"

"Very much, but your own sorrow must be greater. I am so sorry, Deborrah."

Deborrah told Tobie all about the flogging, Jonathan's death and burial, interspersing details about Mary's courage: how she won a mitigation of the sentence, how she cleverly opposed the Roman judge, who was so terribly young. She felt much better talking about it.

Tobie then told both women that he had some gifts for them from Judas and Sadduk and the other Shechem Zealots, but they were down below, he said, still tied to the camel's back. They accepted his invitation to take a much-needed walk.

"Where do you plan to go from here," asked Mary, "now that your work is done in these parts?"

"First, escort you—and Deborrah—to Jerusalem, and then go on to Bethlehem to take up sheep herding again—" He hesitated. "—Unless you have other plans for me." They smiled at each other.

Deborrah, who was up ahead, turned around. "Tobie, is this your horse and camel?"

"The camel is yours, Deborrah," replied Tobie, "compliments of the Zealots. What's more, everything in the bundles is yours, except for the foodstuffs that are mine."

He reached under his cloak, unbuckled a belt, and handed it to Mary. "Something for you, Mary, from Judas of Galilee."

Mary immediately recognized the belt as her own gift to the Zealots. They had returned it, shekels and all, with a note of gratitude and an explanation that they couldn't use the money because they didn't use the advice. They also thought it was an impulsive action on her part, but Mary was quick to deny this. In any case, Tobie would not take it back. After removing two large baskets of foodstuffs from the camel's back, Tobie led the way to the quadrangle where there were several open fires. They made themselves comfortable at one of them; then he began to remove the most extraordinary food—loaves of wheat bread, dressed chicken, eggs. Seeing these, one of their fellow travelers remarked grandiosely, "Morsels for mortals fit for the Roman Senate! Nice catch, Captain! Where'd ya get it?"

Tobie's face flushed. He was checked. "Romans aren't the only people who eat chicken and eggs in Palestine. Tonight you, too, my friend, shall indulge. Here," he said as he reached over for an exquisitely-shaped Grecian bottle of wine, "Drink to your heart's content." He stood up, held high a chicken in each of his outstretched hands. "Gifts from the Romans for the oppressed Jew. Come and get it!" Then another bottle of wine and another, fruit and honey cakes, imported nuts, dried vegetables, and choice spices... another log on the fire, another bottle of wine. The eggs were boiled, scrambled, fried, and mixed raw with wine, but always with wine. Tobie drank his favorite, the deep purple wine of Galilee.

There was singing and dancing as the fervor of festivities mounted, and as always a few individuals showed they couldn't take the pace. A tall Bedouin shouted, "Down with the uncircumcised pigs from Rome, but thank Jove for chicken!" Another, dancing only with his bottle, kept saying, "To Sheol with you, Herod, you foreign jackass!" Tobie sensed the trend to fight rather than to romance. He stood up and, waving a bottle of his own, urged everyone to dance and sing.

Mary leaned over to Deborrah and put her arm around

her. "It's time for putting my baby to bed. Care to join me?"

"Yes, but where's the baby?" asked Deborrah as they walked off into the darkness.

When Tobie discovered that Mary and Deborrah had gone, he let himself go along with the crowd until the baskets and bottles were empty. Empty baskets, empty bottles, no people, a dying fire, and Tobie all alone, abashed in the sudden flood of moonlight that came from over the roof of the caravanserai in the direction of Mt. Gerizim. The moon was mad last night, tonight it seemed vengeful...all was taken away. Last night he ran, tonight he was at a standstill. He picked up an ornate empty Grecian bottle, gazed at it momentarily, then dashed it into the glowing embers, scattering them explosively.

"Tobie..." came the soft call from the loggia. "Tobie, look up here."

"Why should I?" he kept on staring into the fire.

"Here is a message for you," continued the voice.

Tobie looked up just in time to catch the note rolled tightly into a ring; then slipping the ring on his finger, he read in the light of the many-faced moon:

"Dear Tobie:
        Everybody loves you,
        let me tell you who.
        Mary loves you,
        thinks you are great,
        greater than great.
        Deborrah loves you,
        you are her hero,
        a man of super worth.
        Jesus the Messiah
        your secret friend
        unborn but knowing
        loves you.
        Everybody loves you—
        except maybe you—
        but that's your own fault....
        You need hope.
        Say it to God,

say it to yourself,
'I have hope in the ones I love,'
Tomorrow is another day,
Now get some rest!

Mary."

Mary lay awake, sharing Tobie's mental anguish. She felt that his burden was heavier than hers, for he didn't have her consolations. She could recall Gabriel's words; she had her baby. She prayed that God would send him Gabriel, yes, even tonight.... What was it Tobie said about Joseph? How could he believe in me now that I will have been away from home so long? How long? Dear God. Poor Miriam! No wonder she jumped off the Eastcliff. Tobie lives in Bethlehem. He said he believes in me—but I'm going to Ain Karim. But then what? Back to Nazareth? Gabriel, come back to me. I need you. My body is trembling. Why am I perspiring so? I'm cold! Why did I leave Mama and Papa? Mama gave Papa saffron mixed with crocus—the vivid yellow Karkom, antispasmodic potion.... Tobie took wine.... Anemone is sweet. I can smell it. It's on the table... it's in my hand.... Will it help me forget? Please, God, NO!... What?... Gabriel no more? Now Zachary? Go to Zachary? Let it be done now not for me, but for my baby. Let it be...."

Chapter 11

One of the twenty thousand clergymen ordained to serve the Temple in Jerusalem was Mary's cousin, Zachary, an elderly priest of the distinguished class of Abia which dated back a thousand years in Jewish history to King David. Although Zachary belonged to no political sect, he nevertheless, as a good Jew, opposed the octopus-like strangling imperialism of Rome. Every red-blooded man has convictions and principles which come to act in the face of challenge. If Zachary weren't a priest, he would be a leading Zealot.

Unfortunately, a gap greater than the Dead Sea existed between the people who visited the Temple and its priesthood. Wittingly or unwittingly, they were unable to fill the empty stomachs of Herod's slaves, who showed little taste for true religious expression. Bloated stomachs have little energy. Caught between Herod and Rome, priests themselves were on the defensive and discredited. The pseudo-sacred religionists took religion into their own hands and rationalized their own truths and dogmas. They counted

numbers, like "every tenth one goes to the temple"; they
weighed ounces of food and called it "penance"; they
measured miles and called it "the Sabbath" or "the Lord's
Day." This kind of activism, they called religion.

Mary's body sheltered the little Person who in His public
ministry would categorize these people as hypocrites and
whited sepulchers (Mt. 23:27). They lacked the interior life
of God's grace which gives strength to mind and body.

Cousin Zachary served these people enslaved by
militarism, impoverished by excessive taxation, and confused
by a clergy unable to help even if it were capable. Often
Zachary confided to his wife, Elizabeth, that he enjoyed
greater genuine devotion at home than he did at the Temple. He considered it his good fortune that he, like all priests
of his class, was called upon to serve in the Temple only
one week out of twenty-four. There were twenty-four classes,
and each served in turn. However little work this was, the
priest was amply rewarded with a share in the offerings and
sacrifices brought to the Temple. Because of his excellent
seniority status, Zachary would be favored with assignments
on the important feast days, such as the Passover, Feast of
Weeks, Purim, or Yom Kippur, to which people came from
all of Palestine and beyond from the great diaspora.

It was in late September on the tenth day of the Hebrew
month of Tishri on the most solemn day of the Jewish calen-
dar, Yom Kippur, the Day of Forgiveness or Atonement,
that Mary's Cousin Zachary, the priest, was met by Gabriel,
the same messenger of God who appeared to Mary six
months later. He was told that he and his wife Elizabeth,
both in advanced years, would conceive a son to be named
"John," whom people would call the Baptizer. This was
the best news the old priest had ever heard in over forty-
nine years of priesthood, especially because he was childless,
and in the current lingo of the Temple area, "a childless
man should be thought of as dead."

The overpowering feeling of begetting a son gave new purpose to Zachary's anticipated act of love with Elizabeth,
which had become almost nonexistent. He felt a sense of
levitation permeate the masculinity of his ego. He became
anxious. There was no doubt in his own mind that he could

do it, but he wondered about "poor Beth," at her age, in her late sixties—how could she carry a child for nine months and survive? Gabriel waited for Zachary's word of acceptance. And because all this was taking place within the Holy of Holies where the priest and the angel were alone, the congregation outside likewise had gone into a holding attitude. Heaven and earth waited. Finally Gabriel laid it on the line for him: "Listen!" he said. *"Since you have not believed my words, which will come true at their appointed time, you will be silenced and have no power of speech until this has happened"* (Lk. 1:20).

The nine days of Yom Kippur, days of repentance, ended abruptly for the people in attendance, but for Zachary they were a prelude to a Yom Kippur that would last nine months, months of silence before he would again hear himself say, "John." He had two explanations to make to his wife on his return home that night, one that he was unable to speak, and the other that an angelic conception was in order. Neither proved easy.

The sign that came to Elizabeth was more manifest; shortly thereafter she knew she was pregnant, but the fact only emphasized her previous barrenness, so that she withdrew for five months into the hidden recesses of her home and vineyard. She prayed in thankfulness to the Lord, for he removed from her the humiliation she suffered among her relatives, friends, and Temple associates. Something inside her however kept her from showing it. In her day particularly, and too often in too many other times as well, women were blamed for a childless marriage. Elizabeth was impressed with this notion, and she felt others would be reminded of it. Also there was a sense of shame in being pregnant at her age—old people were thought not to do these things. It was very much apparent after five months that God through the Zachary couple had struck out this notion.

As the genial and loving Elizabeth became accustomed to carrying her unborn child, so too Zachary became proficient in making his thoughts known by using a tablet and stylus. Neither was any longer embarrassed by their needful preoccupation. One day in early April, while Zachary and his vineyard foreman were examining the spring growth

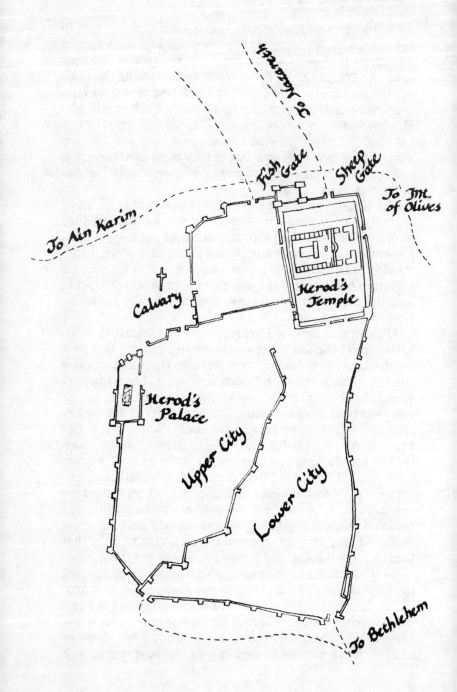

of the vines at the far end of the rocky hillside, he suddenly stood erect and pointed over the northern ridge into the blue sky.

"It might be one of our pigeons," suggested Darion, the foreman.

Keenness of sight compensated for a silent larynx, and Zachary kept nodding his head as he continued to jab into the sky.

"Alexander!" cried Darion. "His flight pattern is always over the lower region of the ridge."

Zachary and Darion beat the household to the loft because of their proximity, while the graceful wings of the champion soared around aloft and gradually fluttered to rest on the peak of the roof. Zachary reached out with cupped hands and Alexander proudly stepped in. He first fondled the tired messenger, calming it, then carefully removed the delicate encasement. Inside he found the tiny roll of onion-skin-like paper on which was written in heavy hand:

"Joachim is dead. All pigeons Mary took with her returned same time. She must be in serious trouble. Please find her. Anna remains in shock.

Joseph"

Zachary came down from the loft, handed the message to Darion, then dropped to his knees and commended the soul of his cousin, Joachim, to his Maker. Darion joined him, but the solemnity of the occasion prompted him to pray in the idiom of his own native Macedonia. Alexander, almost home, rigid on his perch, looked down upon the familiar white-haired old man kneeling next to the dark-haired young Greek, but this time he sensed that what he brought was bad news.

Moments later, Elizabeth, not unlike the saddened wife of Lot, read the message and turned stone cold. "Zachary," she urged, "You must leave immediately for the Temple and find Mary. Take Aaron with you—he knows his way around the city and the Temple and will drive you."

* * * * * * *

"The daughter of Joachim is nowhere to be found," said Aaron despondently to his Master, who had been waiting

long and patiently. "I've asked everyone and looked
everywhere in the Temple area."

"She's not here," scrolled Zachary, stating the obvious.

"What now, Rabban?"

Zachary mustered energy enough to smile at Aaron in
satisfaction of his use of the flattering term, "Rabban,"
one which was used only for the great rabbinical dignitaries
who reached the distinguished heights of leadership in the
Sanhedrin. He knew he wasn't entitled to it, but it was obvious the white-haired old man enjoyed hearing it and encouraged its use.

"Rabban," asked Aaron, "do you wish to start for
home?"

Occasionally a fellow priest passed by and warmly greeted
Zachary and his young Levite. At first, Zachary felt uneasy
being there, for he knew that everyone had discussed his
encounter with the angel and his subsequent censure. Most
priests, though, had their own problems and hurried by
without much more than a fraternal "Shalom."

Aaron could see that Zachary's thoughts were far away.
The smile was gone. Mary was gone. Was this a further
punishment in the Almighty's divine plan? He reached under
his arm and helped him up from the cold stone bench. "Let's
walk toward the Nicanor Gate," suggested Aaron. "We'll
search for Mary as we go. The carriage is parked behind
the slaughter house of the Temple."

From the peaceful serenity of the Priests' Court, the two
men passed through the narrows between Solomon's Porch
and the Sanhedrin, and as they walked they could hear the
bleating and lowing of the animals and the shouting of men.
They followed behind this traffic which led to the unloading
places at the slaughter house. They now could smell the
heavy air of burning fat, the stench of entrails, and fresh
dung. The wicked world emits a terminal putrefaction in
violence as it approaches the thresholds of divinity. It happens to trash when it is subjected to the change into energy,
or it is the appearance of the natural when converted to
divine life. Aaron remarked: " *The Lord gave, the Lord
has taken back. Blessed be the name of the Lord'* (Job 1:21).
For those good people who gave in sacrifice, and believed

in their giving, the Lord will not be outdone in generosity. They shall share in the final outcome 'double what they had before'."

Homeward bound, Aaron guided Ebal the faithful mule and the cumbersome carriage through a maze of narrow streets. "I hope you don't mind, Rabban, but we're going to leave the city by way of the Fish Gate," Aaron broke the gloomy silence. "I missed the turn to the Ephraim Gate."

In the hours before twilight, everyone seemed in a rush to get inside the city, and especially from the north where traffic was the heaviest. Bangling carts, animals, and people on horseback, on camels, and on foot poured through the Fish Gate like grain through a funnel. In the face of this onrush Ebal and his carriage made no headway; he soon found himself to one side waiting for a break. It came when a slow-moving cart pulled by a team of heavy oxen delayed traffic so that Ebal with a snap of the reins from Aaron made a run for it. As he did, the rear wheel of the carriage struck the bean-pole leg of a tall camel coming around the oxen, causing it to stumble and fall to its knees. The carriage swerved so that it formed a perfect barrier from wall to wall of the gate. There was shouting and cursing. A young man on horseback shouted at Aaron, "Where in hades are you and that jackass going?" Traffic began to back up in both directions. The crowd gathered.

"Mary!" cried Zachary within himself, as he leaped from the carriage in front of the kneeling camel.

Tobie on horseback was about to strike him down, when Mary cried, "Don't, Tobie! It's Cousin Zachary!" She slid down the camel's side, landed on her feet and into the arms of her waiting cousin.

Nearby some fool yelled, "Get moving! If you want to make love, get off the highway."

Quickly Mary's paraphernalia passed from Deborrah, still on the camel's back, to Tobie on horseback and then to Aaron, who placed it into the carriage. Tobie took the camel's reins and led the injured animal aside, while the carriage was righted, and he soon became lost in the rush out of the city. Tobie and Mary, who had wondered how they would say good-bye upon parting in Jerusalem, now found

themselves carried by the human stream in different directions. They felt cheated.

As Mary sat silently, amazed, thanking God for Tobie,
she felt a gentle tapping on her hand. She looked up at
Zachary and beheld a smile of deep understanding. She
moved a little closer to him, saying, "Sorry, my dear cousin.
I'd forgotten that you can't talk."

"It's four miles to Ain Karim," said Aaron. "I hope you
and your baby manage all right."

"I didn't think you knew, Aaron," said Mary, surprised.

"Alexander told me."

"Aaron is part of the family," wrote Zachary on his
bumping tablet.

"And may I ask," said Mary to Zachary, "how is Cousin
Elizabeth and her child of six months?"

"Didn't think you knew, Mary," said Aaron from the
driver's seat.

"Gabriel himself told me," answered Mary. "Strangely, at first I couldn't understand why he would tell me this
statistic, but as time went on, it has become a key factor
in my faith."

"Rabban and Elizabeth have been very happy ever since."

"How nice of you to call Cousin Zachary 'Rabban,' "
said Mary. "Papa often said that he could have attained
the title deservedly by rising to the heights of leadership in
the Sanhedrin, but he was childless. Elizabeth too felt guilty about it and withdrew from meeting people."

"No one knows better than Zachary and Elizabeth," said
Aaron, "that they wanted to have children, for voluntary
childlessness is a horrible crime among our people. Even
more so, voluntary celibacy is punishable by death.
Remember how Isaiah denounced King Hezekiah by sternly reminding him that the penalty for childlessness is death?"

Zachary attempted to write on his tablet as the hips of
the carriage rebounded over the rough road in an unpredict-
able manner. Finally in disgust, he motioned to Aaron to
stop, and he pointed to a spot along the roadside. Mary
watched him write: "cf. Ps. 127:3."

"I know what that is," said Mary.

"It's a reference to one of the songs of ascent by

Solomon,'' said Aaron, "and speaks of the fruit of the
womb as a reward."

Aaron looked at Mary. Slowly she said, "Lo, sons are
a heritage from the Lord, the fruit of the womb a reward."

Zachary clapped his hands, patted Mary on the back, then
pushed Aaron on the shoulder as if to discard him. Aaron
only spoke to Ebal, "Move on," as he snapped the reins.

"Just a minute," pleaded Mary. "Since it was no fault
of your own nor Elizabeth's that you did not have children,
why did the messenger Gabriel see fit to deprive you of your
speech?"

Zachary cocked his head, raised his open palms outward,
and looked a picture of helplessness. He then motioned
Aaron to speak.

"Rabban uses me for his mouthpiece. I was with him
when it all happened, Mary. I was leading the people in song,
while Rabban was in the inner sanctuary, doing the rite of
incensations. I had a premonition that something happened
to him; we had sung psalms until the candles burned down.
The people were restless. I went to the curtain shielding him
from us, gradually pulled it aside to look in, and behold,
I heard a strange voice saying, *'My name is Gabriel. My
place is in God's presence. I have been sent here to tell you
that you shall father a son. How can you say to me that
this is impossible? Let these be your last words until what
I have told you is accomplished'* '' (Lk. 1:19).

"But this only tells us that it happened," said Mary. "But
why? Why punish Zachary?"

"As Rabban told me, he asked the messenger how it could
happen that such an old couple as Elizabeth and himself
could conceive and how she could carry a child for nine
months in her weary frame."

"I'm reminded," said Mary, "that I asked Gabriel the
same thing. 'How can it be that I would become pregnant
without a man?' The messenger didn't seem disturbed with
me. He told me the Holy Spirit would do everything."

"Yours was different," answered Aaron. "You were willing, and you believed it would happen, but you were asking for further instructions as to how the messenger wanted
you to do it. With Zachary, he being a priest and husband,

he ought to have had enough faith, and know-how, to make things work. Right, Rabban?'' appealed Aaron.

Zachary kept nodding his head.

''Rabban himself told me that Gabriel declared to him that 'because you did not believe my words...you will be unable to speak.' ''

Zachary held his tablet in front of Mary. ''I didn't think angels were so sensitive. I was only asking for a sign. The one I got, I don't like.''

''Rabban,'' Mary observed kindly, ''your infirmity is Elizabeth's strength. In this you can glory. Your task with her is much greater. Your loss is worth a thousand words to her.''

Zachary placed his hand on Mary's.

Chapter 12

"There goes Alexander!" shouted Aaron as the carriage drove into the beautiful, spacious grounds of the Zachary homestead. The champion carrier shot out of the loft as from a sling and bolted straight for the lower section of the northern ridge. "Well timed, Darion," continued Aaron. "Your instructions were followed to the letter, Rabban. He's off to Nazareth on the first sight of Mary."

"Did Alexander fly here with the two other pigeons?" asked Mary.

"No," said Aaron, "he came to us from Nazareth." (But, he thought, this is not the time to tell about Joachim.) "Look," he added, "the entire household stands at the entrance to greet you."

A cheer went up led by Cousin Elizabeth as she ran to the carriage to greet Mary, returned to them from the unknown. *"My, how tall you've grown! But, tell me, why does the mother of my Lord pay us the honor of a visit?"*

Mary answered, *"Though I come from poor Galilee, my innermost being bears the life of God! Generations shall be blessed with the fruit of my womb! Gabriel told me so."*

"When we embraced, my own baby jumped at Yours—

Yours is the reason for my miracle, and therefore Yours must be the greater one," responded Elizabeth.

Mary explained, *"The promise of the prophets has been fulfilled. God has exalted the lowly and has scattered princes. Those who hunger shall be filled. Those who have all shall hunger."*

"Though you are young enough to be my daughter," said Elizabeth, *"you are old enough to be my equal in the sons that God has made."*

Mary assured her, *"God has kept his promises made to our fathers. I have come to live in the shadow of your example."*

No one moved. Even the children remained transfixed by the mysticism of the moment. They hung on each word, even though it was not completely understood. Back to reality came the voice of Elizabeth. "Mary, this is Darion, the vineyard foreman, his wife and four children. And here are Aaron's wife and three children; Cassandra, who keeps all of us healthy with her cooking; and her husband, Esau, who fixes everything from headaches to horsehoofs." Nimbly, Elizabeth shooed away two cats and a dog, calling them by name as she led her family into the house.

All passed through the family chapel and then into the large dining room. "Cassandra knew right along that you would be here today, Mary," said Elizabeth. "She has emptied the cupboards. Please be seated."

At that moment Cassandra walked in with a huge tray of fluffy white fish with rings and rings of sliced onion. "Eat when you're hungry, drink when you're thirsty," she repeated from the tractate Berakoth.

"Can't you think of something different for the occasion?" said Aaron. Then he turned to Mary. "She justifies the hours of mealtime with this no matter at what hour we eat. Hope you're hungry?"

"Starving!" exclaimed Mary. She turned to Elizabeth. "Forgive me for telling the truth."

"In this house, the truth is sacred," responded Elizabeth. All ate heartily, and Elizabeth began to fidget as though she just lost her appetite—which she probably did. She looked at Zachary—he wouldn't say it . . . Aaron? Darion?

It's been delayed long enough. "Mary," she said, tenderly, "we received the sad news of Papa's death Tuesday. It was his heart. The note was signed by Joseph—"

"Oh, no, dear Papa!" Mary covered her face with her hands. A deep silence jelled everything. Mary kept wiping away a flow of tears from her nose and cheeks. "He is with Yahweh!"

"Joseph will look after Mama and the place. Don't worry," said Elizabeth.

"I wonder," said Mary, thinking aloud, "I wonder if I hastened his death?"

"How could you?" said Aaron, "You weren't there."

"That's just it. I should have been."

"Your absence was not of your doing," added Elizabeth.

"I should have been there when all those pigeons arrived at the same time. Then Papa wouldn't have been shocked."

"What pigeons?" asked Aaron.

Mary went on to tell about the attack at Shechem and how the crate that held the homing pigeons was demolished and they all flew off at the same time. It must have shocked Papa to see them so that he never recovered.

Zachary handed Mary his table of wax upon which he had written: "Joy built a bridge between us today, now let sorrow walk across it."

"Thanks Rabban. My loss of a father has been lessened, for I have gained you—" she looked at Elizabeth, "and another mother," and at Aaron "and a brother." To all she said, "And a beautiful, large family.

The rigors of the journey, the traumatic accident at the Fish Gate, the gamut of emotions with Cousin Zachary, his place and family, the encounter with aging Elizabeth, the death of Papa, and the mysticism of pregnancy all had exhausted her. Now she was alone in her tidy room limited only by her unlimited thoughts and racing emotions. She walked up to the window; it was barred. Not a star in the heavens—all was pitch black. In her room a tiny oil lamp on the wall accentuated the darkness. She stared at it. She wondered. The Shemonah Esreh, that night prayer which fixed her position with God, came automatically to her lips. She was clutching to hold on. She felt like she was drifting, insecure. Where was the immovable point of origin, the identifiable father of love? Every pregnant woman needs a man. "Have I lost Joseph? Why did I leave him? Will he disown my baby? He's not the father. Who will speak up for me?"

When in her night prayer she began the Benedictions, everything she mentioned in blessing appeared to disintegrate, become detached, fall away; the leaves were falling in the wind, raindrops kept falling hard on her face, huge rocks came tumbling down the mountain side; they all kept dumping on an olive grove which contained a fresh grave. "Papa, it's all gone. . . . Come back, I need you. Hold my hand, help me climb above these falling things—now, tonight."

After a moment, the falling insecurities all stopped. She was in a cave with Jeremiah, Ezekiel, Isaiah, Daniel, but no one spoke. It was damp and cold; her aloneness was accented. The others offered no comfort; they sat in a fixed position. Only the wind howled about the entrance. "Speak, someone!" cried Mary. "Tell me what I must do. My baby grows within me, both of us will be stoned." Then there was Zachary standing in back of the prophets, yes, it was Cousin Zachary, "Rabban"—he would speak. She listened. But he was speechless.

Like the sharp noises of a moving avalanche in the silence of high mountains or the deep creaking of a monstrous Leviathan approaching its docking, Mary felt herself grow inside. She felt the movements; she recognized the sounds. It frightened her. "I'm a girl, now pregnant. A woman, about to be a mother. Alone, and yet—a majority with God. I'm becoming a mother to my child. My Father is. . .ah. . . my husband. . .that is, the Holy Spirit." Mary continued her night prayer, which wasn't literal tonight, for her thoughts were one thing and words another. Finally, in place of the last few Benedictions, she mechanically slipped into her own overriding words: "I will have my baby! His name is Jesus. I will run through falling rocks, moor my ship, jump out of childhood, and shout from the rooftops that I am a grown woman, a mother, the source of life and power and love." She fell back on her pillow; the prayer and the wrestling were coming to an end. "O God of Israel, if You are

One, then are you, too, alone? I am alone, make me one with You." Alone, while the whole world waited and yawned.

* * * * * * *

It was exactly a week since Mary's arrival in Ain Karim when the intensive festivities of the Passover and the Week of Unleavened Bread began. The celebration would not only mark the glorious liberation of the Jews from the bondage of the Egyptians, but it would bring into the house of Zachary a guest who played an important role in the liberation of Mary from Judaean politics.

Zachary's entire household was involved in the preparations, and each was instructed to invite someone they knew who would be alone that day, or who was too poor to observe the day with proper ceremony. The generosity of this Temple priest was widespread not alone at the Passover, but for the many Jewish traditional Holy Days. His home at times contained 150 guests. The stucco building was shaped like the letter "U," with a garden patio inside opened at the end into an expansive and neatly-manicured vineyard.

One could readily suppose that Cassandra, the large but gentle Cassandra, would balk at all the extra work, but even with little help, she thrived on it. Her secret was a simple one: good food and plenty of it. Aaron supervised the ritualistic aspects of the feast, for which he was highly qualified, being a Levite. His psychology was to give everyone a part to play, making it seem a game to the young ones and to the circumcised foreigner, Darion, and his family.

The day before the big ceremony when the guests were to arrive, Aaron, while working with Mary in the patio, said, "Mary, have you heard the big news? A genuine Rabban is coming tomorrow to the Passover meal."

"Really?" Mary was not sure just what to say.

"None other than Rabban Hammasiah, the greatest. He is a doctor of Law, an outstanding Scribe, and conversant with King Herod and Rome. He is a member of the Sanhedrin."

"All that," said Mary. "I hope I don't have to meet him."

"He is free to come," continued Aaron, "for his children are grown, his wife is dead, he lives alone. It's delightful to hear him talk. When he's loud he bellows, sending fear into the hearts of listeners. And then when he's soft, he speaks in large, dulcet tones, enrapturing one into submission. He's gracious, entertaining, and most charming."

"Has he ever been here before?" she asked.

"No," replied Aaron. "It'll be the first time."

Mary had a premonition just then that the dignitary was coming to see her. "I hope not," she said, aloud.

"But of course," insisted Aaron, "it *is* the first time."

* * * * * * *

The master bedroom was located adjacent to the family chapel, where Zachary and Elizabeth found respite from their daily cares and communicated with their God. They went there together, or alone. They respected each other's privacy. If Zachary wished to pray alone, he closed the chapel door. No questions were asked. As a priest, he made the chapel central to his style of living.

Tonight, on the even of the Passover, this elderly twosome moved around each other, making an effort to resolve the matter of their Cousin Mary's presence.

"Why isn't she with Joseph?" wrote Zachary on his wax tablet.

"She's afraid to tell him she's pregnant," replied Elizabeth.

"Why afraid?"

"Because he's not the father, you fool."

"Beth, do you really believe it was the Holy Spirit?"

"Careful, husband, Gabriel is liable to deprive you of your hearing next. Of course I believe it. It's not Joseph. Who else?"

"It would be tragic for Mary to have her baby in Nazareth—she'd be stoned before the baby was born." After six months of stylus-tablet conversation with his wife, Zachary had become adept at abbreviating words, just as Elizabeth was good at reading them.

"But if she is carrying the Messiah—he is to be born in Bethlehem—"

"Just a minute," motioned Zachary, as he showed her

the tablet. "Careful, wife, Gabriel is listening!" They laughed, Zachary without a sound.

"Well my own miracle, having your son at my age," said Elizabeth, "makes it easy for me to believe, and to add that I believe He *will* be born as the long line of prophets foretold, in Bethlehem." Elizabeth was standing over Zachary's shoulder.

"Yes," wrote Zachary, "he will in spite of what we do. Let us relax and be inspired by the Holy Spirit to cooperate."

"Then why did you invite Hammasiah?" asked Elizabeth. "Do you intend him to take over?"

"No! But I want to hear what he has to say. This is big."

"You too are a priest, husband, as much as Hammasiah. You ought not shirk your responsibilities, but with faith in God's Providence move with the events step by step. God will give you the grace as you need it."

Zachary had written, "If you say so, my love," somewhat facetiously, but Elizabeth never saw it, for she had blown out the lamp, signaling the conference was over.

* * * * * * *

With the dawn Elizabeth maneuvered to offer a subtle suggestion to Mary. How to tell her? The coarse, unattractive clothes from Galilee must be discarded. Distinguished company was coming; priests and their wives were expected throughout the Week of Unleavened Bread. After breakfast Elizabeth accompanied Mary to her room, casually remarking, "Mary, would you like to see some of the fine fabrics I have acquired over the years? I've been anxious to show them to you. In my condition I've not been wearing them."

"Sounds interesting," said Mary.

They made the turn and in a moment were standing in front of Cousin Elizabeth's wardrobe. After quickly passing over a few decoys, Elizabeth said, "This one is a favorite. It was made for a special occasion a few years ago."

Mary held it full length against her body. "Beautiful!" exclaimed Elizabeth. "It fits you perfectly."

"It might be a little long," observed Mary.

"There is a belt that goes with it—here somewhere. Would you like to try it on, Mary?"

"If you don't mind. It is very pretty." She made the change right there with surprising alacrity. She walked across the room self-consciously, which prompted Elizabeth to say, "Just be yourself, dear girl; you have all the natural charm any woman would envy. Relax and let nature take over."

"Right now I feel a little like a wooden doll. How can I forget that I'm wearing it? It's—it's perfect."

"I would like to give it to you. It's yours, so you needn't feel that you are walking in borrowed clothes. Let it become an extension of yourself."

"I can't take it, Cousin," said Mary. "It's too rich for Joachim's daughter—and when would I wear it?"

"Today, when company comes. You'd be doing me a big favor."

Both women broke out into laughter, threw their arms around each other, and cried.

Chapter 13

"**This is Rabban Hammasiah, Mary,**" said Elizabeth,
"our distinguished guest from Jerusalem."

Mary gave the correct curtsy as her cousin had taught her.
As she did, the verticle pleats in her ankle-length dress flared
at her sides and knees. When she stood up straight, she was
slender and symmetrical as an Iconium pillar of sparkling
blues and reflecting whites. Her garment was a product of
Hellenistic culture, a favorite among Palestine's elite. Her
jet-black hair fell to her shoulders, covering the snug collar
with lacy folds apparent only under her chin. But most of
all there was her plain, unadorned face with jewel-like eyes
relaying her interior beauty.

"Rabban," said Elizabeth, "Mary is our dear cousin from
Nazareth, Joachim's daughter. She is to stay with us for
a while."

"How extremely charming." Rabban Hammasiah bowed
slightly toward Mary.

"Sir, I've been told many wonderful things about you."
Mary was showing some restraint in her new role as socialite.
"I am happy to know you."

"Ummmm...and why haven't I been told about you?"

countered the distinguished Rabban. "I have been denied."

"When the time comes," interjected Elizabeth, "she herself will tell you all there is to know—if you'll be so kind as to lend her your ear."

"My ear, indeed, and I'm afraid she already has my heart."

"Now all we have to know is the time and place," said Elizabeth, making every effort to get to the point. "Mary wishes to consult with you about her problem."

"Is it possible for one so young and replete with beauty to harbor a problem? How would midmorning of Tuesday next suit you ladies?"

After a few amenities, Mary excused herself.

Elizabeth and the great Rabban from the Sanhedrin moved with dignity and grace throughout the spacious grounds. Along with the household, the poor from Ain Karim, friends from Jerusalem, and relatives—some previously unknown to Mary—were all there. Elizabeth was unusually large, or at least seemed so in her copious maternity regalia. She had become proud of her condition, after long-delayed expectations. When confronted all too frequently with the question, "How does it feel to be pregnant at your age?" she responded without variation: "I'm young again!"

"Rabban Hammasiah, would you kindly excuse me? I must announce the beginning of the Passover meal," said Elizabeth after she had presented her guest, "for Zachary is still handicapped."

Aaron, given the signal to invoke God's blessing, intoned: *"Blessed are you, Lord our God, King of the Universe, who has sanctified us by his commandments, and has commanded us to light the festival candle"* (Lv. 23:5; also cf. Nb 28:16, Dt. 16:1).

With another signal from Zachary, who was seated in the middle of the table in the dining room facing the opening to the patio, Aaron now went on to read the Hagadah, which told the story of Moses and the chosen people, who after about two hundred years of slavery in Egypt were then led to freedom.

Darion was next. He brought out the Matzoth, a flat, thin

cake made of flour without yeast or salt. When everyone was served, Zachary motioned that they should eat it. Simultaneously, Elizabeth added, "...in the spirit of penance in commemoration of our forefathers who in their haste took unreadied dough and were forced to eat it in the hot desert."

Some of the children grimaced at the taste.

"I shall bring you out," intoned Aaron. This signalled the first cup of wine, for bondage was no more.

Aaron prayed: "...Moses declared the feasts of God to the children of Israel. Blessed are you, Lord God, King of the Universe, who created the fruit of the vine."

Three more times did Aaron repeat the memento of the Exodus, and three more times did everyone drink to their Liberator.

Just before the fifth intonation, Elizabeth motioned to Aaron to sit down, and she would take over. Many Jews believed it was the favorite prophet Elijah who someday would come at the Passover and announce the coming of the Messiah. Elizabeth now knew better. She directed the usual generous drink of wine to be set on the seder table for Elijah. All glasses were filled. She ordered the gates and doors to be opened for his entrance, if he so wished, and then raising her glass, she said, "There is good news for all Jews this year. A new deliverance! A greater freedom than Moses brought about!" She was about to tell them of her son, John, who would indeed someday be called Elijah, for it was he who would announce the coming of the Messiah. Tears filled her eyes; her throat tightened; she could only say in a whisper, "Now is not the time for the truth. . . . Aaron—bring me Elijah's drink." She drank it to the last sip.

"Sacrilege!" shouted someone in the patio.

"Elizabeth, you overstepped your bounds," whispered Rabban Hammasiah. "No one ever touches Elijah's portion."

"Everyone prepares for someone," spoke Elizabeth loudly. "I'm preparing for my son."

Zachary stood up and himself brought forward the "maror," that bitter dish of sticks of horseradish. As he passed the large platter, he dipped his stick into the charoseth sauce made from wine, apples, and nuts; others followed his example. Darion and his family dipped lightly, for they had been introduced to this awful-tasting concoction, a reminder of the sufferings of their ancestors in religion, only a few short years ago.

When the salt water was passed, Darion the Greek had already tasted his own tears resulting from the horseradish but drank nevertheless to the memory of the tears of those brave people whose tears flowed freely in captivity in Egypt.

They drank and sang merrily to their memories until memories were no more than the scattered skeletal members of the Lamb, picked clean and strewn about. Rabban Zachary, using Aaron as a mouthpiece, thanked all for coming and requested they sing selections on springtime from Solomon's *Song of Songs* while all helped to pick up the leftover fragments and tidy things up.

To the distant chant of a crowd of young people who chose to linger longer in the upper reaches of the vineyard, Mary made her way to her room. "A month ago, I'd have joined them," she said to herself. Now her thoughts were about Papa—and her accelerated maturity: "Wine flowing straight to my Beloved" (Sg. 7:10).

After witnessing Elizabeth's break with tradition, Rabban Hammasiah lectured with renewed enthusiasm in the Temple about the need to observe Judaistic Law. Women, he noted, were inclined to emphasize sentiment, or love, rather than obedience to the Law. There was danger in this, for the object of one's affections could at times be illegal.

"I concur with Rabbi Hillel," stated Hammasiah one day in class, "that 'the Law is the ultimate goal of all education.' This means that if you do love someone, you do it to bring him to the Law."

Although the Rabban's reputation was tarnished lately through personal inconsistencies and his leanings toward the irascible Herod, he nevertheless attracted students from everywhere in the Empire.

"What is the first thing a Jewish lad of five is taught?" he asked. "It is the Law, that is, how to obey. At ten, it is the Mishnah, the oral tradition of the Law. Finally at fifteen, the young one learns the Talmud, the commentary on the Law.''

"Sir," ventured a student from the Highlands, "after all this, doesn't love take over? What then happens to the Law?"

"Judging by your age," responded Hammasiah, "I assume that you use the word love as synonymous with sex. There is a difference: love without purpose is lust. Lust which per se is promiscuous becomes vice. To love the Law is divine; to love a woman is natural. Divine love is dominated by the divine Law, whereas natural love must follow the natural Law. Always the Law!''

Another student added, "From what you say, love is life-giving, but lust destroys either one or both persons of a relationship. It doesn't seem that love need be synonymous with sex."

"Granted," said Hammasiah. "The Law is mindful of this and prescribes that a young man should marry at the age of eighteen, stating that he should be guided to the Chuppa, the bridal chamber. Then, there is more Law: the law of nature, which is the law of God—The summation of all the virtues involved—and total obedience to the Law is love."

"Begging your pardon, Sir," said the Highlander, "you make it sound mechanical, 'duty-full,' if I may coin a word. Can one love the Law as he loves a woman."

"Very much so," answered Rabban. "At the root of love is the common denominator of 'obedience.' True love is obedient to the needs of the beloved. Lasting love is disciplined, which means that it has its laws."

"Are you saying, Sir, that if one obeys the laws of love perfectly, he will then love perfectly?"

"Yes, but only theoretically," said Hammasiah, "for perfection in this life is unattainable. Man only strives for it. It is always merely a goal. In this case, the Law is a means to true love."

"A perfect society," said the student, "would be one in which all persons perfectly obeyed all laws."

"This is true," said Hammasiah, "and this means we would all be living in love with one another. Good logic, but life laughs at logic."

"Not so." The young man was respectful, but his idealism began to show. "I hear the voice of the many prophets who told of the Messiah—his name shall be Emmanuel, and he shall establish a kingdom of love. This will be the new law: 'Love one another' " (cf. Lv. 19:18).

"To consider this in man's development today," observed Rabban, "is sheer nonsense. We are living in an age of 'an eye for an eye, and a tooth for a tooth'—an age of justice" (cf. Ex. 21:24, Mt. 5:38).

"Sir, there are students here from all over Judaea, and beyond, and most of them have heard of the imminence of Emmanuel's birth."

"Enough of this discussion," ruled Rabban. "We are now in the realm of rumors and hearsay. Let us get on with the next topic: 'The Rules and Regulations Governing the Observance of the Sabbath and other Major Feasts.' "

* * * * * * * *

"Shalom, Rabban," said Elizabeth, "we have come to keep our appointment with you."

"How delightful!" said Rabban Hammasiah, extending his hand. "Two charming ladies to see me."

Rabban's home was spacious, but austere. Except for a few servants, he lived alone since the death of his wife. In order to pursue the game of politics, both state and church, he entertained lavishly with cornucopia unseen in the warehouses of his mind and his larder. Among his guests were personages of high rank from the Pharisees, Sadducees, Scribes, and occasionally a leading Roman in the service of his government. Since Rabban was ideologically accommodating to many, he sometimes compromised his own convictions.

"Well, Elizabeth, how did you survive the festivities of the Passover?" asked Rabban. "You were indeed a most gracious hostess."

"Thank you," replied Elizabeth. "We all did well. Everything is fine—Rabban, we know you are a busy man, and we are grateful to you for seeing us. Mary has a problem."

"Would you like to tell us about it, young lady?" asked Rabban.

Mary then related how she was solemnly engaged to Joseph but that she was pregnant by the Holy Spirit, that the angel Gabriel told her she was to give birth to a son whose name shall be "Jesus." She added at the end, "My parents sent me to Ain Karim for fear my pregnancy would be detected in Nazareth."

"Are you claiming that you are to give birth to the long-awaited Messiah?" asked Rabban, with penetrating round eyes and a deep, quizzical smile.

"Yes," said Mary.

"I take it Joseph doesn't know about this?"

"He doesn't."

"You are afraid that people will say your son—or daughter—is illegitimate?"

"*Son,* Sir, and the angel Gabriel called him 'the Son of God,' " answered Mary quickly. "I'm not afraid of his being called illegitimate in human terms."

"The Law states that you could be stoned for adultery," observed Hammasiah.

"Adultery?" asked Mary innocently.

"Yes, Mary," interrupted Elizabeth. "People call it that when it is done outside of wedlock. But have no fear, Cousin. God is the father of your child, and He will provide."

"Are you planning on consummating your solemn relationship with Joseph?" asked Rabban.

"I promised Gabriel I would do whatever God asks me to do. At the present time, I don't know God's will." Mary looked at both Hammasiah and Elizabeth, as if to say, "Would you tell me His plan?"

"I don't believe Joseph will marry you," continued the Rabban, "when he discovers that you are with child, a child not his."

"Sir, you say nothing of the supernatural powers of God. Must I be the one to say that all things are possible with God?" Mary wiped a tear from her cheek. The honeymoon with the Holy Spirit was over, she thought. She was thinking of people now. Harsh, cruel people. The kind who threw stones, swore and spit, had hideous faces. She startled when she heard Rabban Hammasiah state dogmatically: "You shall live at the Temple."

"She can stay with us," said Elizabeth.

"Ain Karim is even smaller than Nazareth," said Rabban, "and has more stones."

"The Temple is not new to me," said Mary. "I've stayed there as a child, through the kindness of Cousin Zachary. I liked it and learned much."

"What do you propose to do with Joseph for eight more months, Rabban?" asked Elizabeth.

"If Joseph claims Mary as his wife," declared Rabban, "we will persuade him of the wisdom of our plan. If he does not, then so much the better for Mary's story. I see no problem."

Mary wasn't ready to give up Joseph as a part of God's will. At this point she felt an uncertainty in her because the Rabban appeared to be triumphant. He made her feel that she was just stolen from the arms of Joseph, sort of, from the tender care of one into the master mind of another. It made her uncomfortable.

"My dear young lady," continued Hammasiah, "it is clear to me now that you belong to Israel, the nation of your forefathers. In you, the Law is being fulfilled. Furthermore, Bethlehem is only five miles from Jerusalem, and we'll see to it that, in accordance with the prophecies, the Messiah will be born there."

"Must she go to the Temple immediately?" asked Elizabeth, not entirely convinced.

"No, but there must be no delay beyond the necessities," Rabban stood up, indicating the end of the interview.

"When would you have us return, Rabban?" asked Elizabeth.

"How about two weeks from today, same time?"

"Thanks," said Elizabeth.

As Rabban Hammasiah escorted them to the door, he asked Elizabeth to remind Zachary that he was bringing with him a very special friend from Rome on the day after tomorrow. "I'm sure Zachary will be delighted to meet him." The wise old fox from the Sanhedrin had found himself a new place to take his distinguished guests. Zachary's place had everything: attractive setting, good food, excellent wine, intelligent conversation—and Mary.

* * * * * * *

Zachary was in his chapel when he heard the clear voice of Darion announcing the approach of Rabban Hammasiah and a Roman dignitary. Here was in miniature the present day society of Palestine; military might of the Roman Empire, Judaism personified, and Hellenistic culture, all moving on a collision course. Most intellectuals sought this kind of course, for it represented reality and challenge.

"Zachary, my friend," said Rabban, "this is Vitellius, Emissary of the Emperor, a guest at Herod's Court."

Zachary bowed, as Aaron spoke, "For my master and his household I extend to you a hearty welcome."

When the group arrived at the large table in the patio, Cassandra was already there with foodstuffs and wine in abundance.

"Sir," said Aaron to Vitellius, "I heard at the Temple the other day that you were here investigating revolutionary activities. It would be interesting to know what you have uncovered."

"Aaron," interjected Rabban Hammasiah, "your question sounds threatening to our guest."

"If it's on his mind," said Vitellius, "let him ask it. What I have uncovered is negligible, but I'm afraid there is much lurking under the surface. If it is checked, it'll help not only the protectors in Rome, but especially the home government to survive."

"Is it that strong?" wondered Aaron.

"The Zealots," continued Vitellius, "although few in number, laid waste the whole Shechem garrison and the caravanserai I was in just a few days ago. They are skilled and courageous."

"It's irrational," said Hammasiah, "to murder Romans when you know we invited them in the person of General Pompey for our own protection."

Zachary felt uncomfortable, not being able to talk, and moreover desirous of changing the subject, so he abruptly stood up and offered all a large platter of cheeses and more wine.

"Excellent body and unsurpassed taste!" commented Vitellius, meeting hospitality with flattery.

Zachary nodded with obvious pleasure while Hammasiah was saying, "Zachary's vineyard draws the sun, and the grape is not harvested here until it ripens on the vine."

"Rabban Hammasiah." It was Aaron's penetrating voice again. "The rumor is you have joined the Sadducees."

"It's true, my young Levite. Indeed you are full of rumors today."

"This one is heating up the priests' section of the Temple like the desert wind," responded Aaron.

"You see," continued Hammasiah, "being a Sadducee will facilitate my work for Church and State. It's the Sadducees who control all administrative offices at the Temple and the Collegia."

"Your efforts for peace at home and abroad," observed Vitellius, "should benefit by this, and Rome will consider your position improved."

"But may I ask," pursued Aaron, "what happens to your basic beliefs in, first, the resurrection; second, the coming of the Messiah, and third, the existence of angels?"

"The Sadducees uphold the Law, and I'm a firm believer of everything in the Law." Hammasiah was being evasive. "As you learned not too long ago in the classroom, it is all contained in the Pentateuch."

Zachary had written something on his slate for Aaron, but when Aaron got it, he thought it was to be read aloud for all to hear: "Love is the Law in this house. Enough, Aaron." All applauded Zachary and laughed at the Levite. However, Aaron persisted. "And in this house we have Greek, Judaean, Galilean, priest, laity, and the poor—"

"Ah, indeed." Hammasiah rose to his feet. "And here comes the fairest of Galileans."

It was Mary, returning from the vineyard where she had been working with others of the household. For a moment she backed off, embarrassed by her appearance. She was wearing a scarf around her head and carrying a large basket.

"The girl from Galilee," declared Vitellius as Aaron was

about to make introductions.

"You know Mary, Sir?" asked Aaron.

"We were both in the battle of Shechem, but I'm afraid we were on opposite sides. You are Mary, the daughter of Joachim of Nazareth, Galilee. Right?" asked Vitellius.

"And you, Sir," said Mary, "are Vitellius, eminent citizen of Rome, Emissary of Augustus, Emperor."

"You sound like you're reading it, Mary," interrupted Aaron.

". . . commissioned to act as sole Judge," went on Mary, "in the trial of the Shechem Six. Signed, Herod, Procurator of Palestine."

"Now I declare *this* court to be in session," bantered Vitellius, "and I plead in behalf of myself for mercy—"

"Where justice is denied, how can mercy survive?" said Mary.

"This is better than any Temple play I've ever seen," encouraged Hammasiah.

"A moment ago, our genial host expressed a universal principle that 'Love is the Law of this house'," pleaded Vitellius. "Assuming you are a member, I shall let my case rest."

"Good people are always at a disadvantage," smiled Mary. The conversation ended as abruptly as it started, catching the onlookers off guard.

"In behalf of your host, may I suggest a walk through the vineyard?" asked Aaron.

"Excellent," said Hammasiah. "Let's see the wine at its source."

As the path narrowed into the entrance, Vitellius delayed going with the group so he could join Mary who remained at the table.

"Come along, Mary," he urged.

"Thank you," she said.

"Have you thought any further about my request to take you to Rome with me?"

"Your people wouldn't accept me except as a Judaean slave."

"Don't be difficult."

"Sorry, I should have taken you seriously," said Mary.

"I'm asking you to come as my wife, to speak plainly," said Vitellius.

"I'm trying to avoid the question. Don't you see?"

"But why?"

"I am solemnly bound to Joseph, the carpenter, in Nazareth," she explained. "Our Judaic laws are very strict about this."

"Do you really love him?"

"Must you know all this?"

"Yes, please, for I have influence and can arrange a dissolution of your bond."

"I love Joseph in the sense of duty, submissiveness, and security—not that I have 'fallen in love' with him. Our opportunities for this are at a minimum. I love him in the sense that we both share the same love of God. I feel a relationship of unity with him. It's not easy to explain."

"You do very well," replied Vitellius.

Mary was on the point of telling Vitellius more—about the Holy Spirit, about Jesus—but she was spared all that when he said, "Mary, I'll always cherish a fond memory in my heart for you. If ever there is anything I can do for you, please let me know, and I'll come running."

"Not as a judge," Mary smiled.

"I was unwittingly made an accomplice of Israel's king."

They now joined the group standing in admiration of the beautiful, expansive Sorek River Valley looking westward. The small tributaries formed a many-fingered fan of green dotted with gems of white homes of limestone and alabaster. Zachary's neatly-terraced vineyard faced the long afternoons of the setting sun over the Mediterranean which gently warmed the cheeks of the ripening grapes. Today however, it was late, late spring, and the vines and leaves were not yet fully grown.

* * * * * * *

The next morning following breakfast, Elizabeth invited Mary to take a walk with her "up to the pigeon roost and back." The sun hadn't dissipated the morning fog yet, and it was a bit chilly, so after a trip to their rooms to pick up something warm to wear, they set out.

"Sunshine always wins out in Ain Karim," said Elizabeth, joining Mary. "Start in the fog, finish in the sun."

"You can say that about many things," added Mary. "I think I'm still in the fog about much of my life."

"Don't lose faith with your Maker—He doesn't tell you everything to start with."

"Mind if I ask you a personal question, Cousin?" asked Mary.

"Speak from your heart, Mary—anything"

"When your baby was a month old, did you feel sick, like a little dizzy, upset stomach. I do, especially in the mornings."

"Many mothers do. I did." Elizabeth was anxious to assist this young girl forty years her junior. "Fatigue toward the end of the day can bring it on also."

"Papa used to tell me stories about the sea. It's a little like being seasick—probably not as bad."

"Which reminds me. You know our Jewish men, the story goes, used to leave most of their seagoing enterprises to the Phoenicians, because they dreaded seasickness. Wouldn't it be just grand if we Jewish women could find a country of females who would experience the nausea of childbearing for us? We could go on having our babies and feel liberated."

"I guess I'll try to ignore it," said Mary.

"If you can, and generally you can."

"What if it prevents you from eating?"

"The only danger is lack of nourishment for the baby. Remember what you eat, the baby eats, and if you don't eat, the baby doesn't eat."

"That would be bad over a long period of time," said Mary.

"If you can't eat over a long period, you become weak, and then your baby would be born prematurely, and in a weakened condition. If eating is a problem, it would be well to talk it over with a midwife."

"Another thing, Cousin," said Mary, "does everyone have that awful feeling of bigness, sort of fullness, in other parts of one's body besides the stomach, as early as I am?"

"Oh, sure," chuckled Elizabeth. "Even at my age, my

breasts seem filled, my hips expanded, and I wonder whether I'll get through some of the doorways around here." They laughed at themselves. Elizabeth continued, "Today, my abdomen is touching my ribcage. John seems to be growing outward, rather than up or down, as though he knows he's crowding my heart and lungs. This is the time when it really begins to show."

"You talk about your baby, call him by name, as if he is real," said Mary.

"He is real."

"I guess I meant as if he were present as a person."

"Mary, I'm surprised at you. He is a real, present, person, but living in another world different than ours."

"I talk to Jesus. Sometimes, I think he talks to me," said Mary.

"You're still too much the daughter, not enough the mother," advised Elizabeth. "Too much fear, not enough love! It's all a part of growing up—from receiving everything in life as a daughter to giving everything as a mother. Nature tries to prepare us for this day from the very first moment we fondle a little rag doll to the time we hold flesh and blood in our arms. It has been reassuring to me to think that having a baby is something that has been going on since the creation of women, and I am but a tiny silver link in that chain."

"But you are the object of God's miracle, Cousin," observed Mary, "and you must feel especially protected by Him."

"Not really. He got me started, but in a way I've been acting naturally since, kind of as though I'm on my own. In a way every girl is co-creating with God and is protected by Him. God needs us, too!"

"I believe that," said Mary. "But why is it that joy must be punctured with sorrow, gain preceded by pain? A laugh brings a tear, every gift has a price tag."

"You're kind of young to be talking like that, Mary. Are you worried about something, or have you been hurt?"

"I'm worried about Joseph."

"Joseph? I thought Rabban Hammasiah took care of Joseph. He sent him down the river Nile with a lily in his hand.''

"Cousin Elizabeth, I didn't think you'd ever say such a thing. Maybe that's what the Rabban did, but I don't think that's what Joseph will do.''

Mary and Elizabeth had much to talk about, but when they reached the far side of the vineyard, Elizabeth was tired and suggested they sit. In the peaceful silence four hearts beat as one, and yet each could feel its own beat, Elizabeth and her John, Mary and her Jesus, bound together in the common denominator of their God and His purpose. Just as each clean, white house that dotted the checkered mountain slopes around them contains precious living persons, so too did these two women hold life in the chambers beneath their hearts. It was a time for listening: a gurgling and splashing in the fast-moving waters of a small tributary nearby spoke the need for haste in greening the valley below. The atmosphere was charged with new life.

"People in Ain Karim have much more comfort than in Nazareth,'' reflected Mary.

"I'm afraid they have spent much more time perfecting their surroundings than they have their interior lives. Man builds perfection externally only to find that his capacity to enjoy it has withered in the building process. Zachary has a favorite phrase for this,'' continued Elizabeth; "he calls it 'ego suicide.' ''

"It doesn't help to change boulders into bread?'' asked Mary.

"It didn't do much for our ancestors in the desert to have manna drop from heaven for them.''

"What is the answer?'' pursued Mary.

"It's hidden deep within each man's self-worth. Maybe someday it will surface and we'll know more.''

"You must be tired, Elizabeth,'' suggested Mary. "Shall we go back to the house?''

Cassandra, anticipating the women's return, had prepared a midmorning snack in the grape arbor next to the kitchen. "Nourishment for four !'' she said with a sly grin. On a small, clean white tablecloth, there were jasmine sweetmeats—only two cups, of course—and a pitcher of fresh goat's milk.

After Cassandra excused herself, leaving the women enjoying their refreshments, Elizabeth, deep in thought, began hesitantly, "Mary, you've got to be completely honest with me, and tell me—was it really and truly the Holy Spirit that fathered your child? Sure it wasn't Joseph? Or...?"

"Elizabeth. Believe me, Cousin, I have never slept with any man anytime, in all my life." Mary's face was suddenly reddening, and she was obviously self-conscious. "Not even with Joseph to whom I am promised, as you know (Mt. 1:25). He and Papa were making plans for me to move in with him and start living as man and wife, but all of a sudden, Papa decided I should come here."

"We're glad you're here, and we'll take good care of you, my dear," said Elizabeth, readying her next question. "Girls don't know for sure that they are pregnant as early as you did in your case. It's two, three months sometimes. Just what makes you so sure, so early?"

"I knew it because Gabriel told me," answered Mary.

"Is it that simple?"

"There needn't be anything more, but there was," continued Mary. "Moments after he told me, there was sensation throughout the length and breadth of my whole person. I felt like I was being buoyed up. Everything was pulsating within me. When I became aware of my surroundings, I was prostrate in prayer."

"Did Gabriel give you any instructions which might help us in caring for you and your baby?" asked Elizabeth.

"Oh, yes," said Mary. "He told me that I should call the child 'Jesus,' and that he will be called 'Son of God.' Also he told me about you, Cousin, that you were six months with child in spite of your age, and that you had been barren—"

"I'm not sure it was necessary for him to say all that about me," said Elizabeth with her chuckle, "but this must have given you an idea that he wanted you to come to stay with us."

"That's the way it worked out," said Mary. "It's comforting to be here."

"In three months your pregnancy will be more apparent, and we'll know more about it," said Elizabeth. "There'll be physical signs."

"Does that mean you don't believe me now, Cousin?"

"Yes, I do believe you. Even if I didn't know you, why would you travel three days, leave home, and come here just to tell me a lie?"

"To believe is a gift of God."

"Good people help."

"Can you imagine what people will say," said Mary, "when they find out I'm pregnant and not living with Joseph?"

"And imagine what they'll say about an old woman getting herself pregnant—it'll take more than faith in both cases."

"God isn't telling us everything," pondered Mary.

"Well, I'm telling everybody what God has done for me. My flags are all hoisted and waving. I've wasted five months in hiding, and now I'm ashamed of being ashamed. No more. I still have the traces of the red blotch between my eyes," said Elizabeth pointing to the top of the bridge of her nose. "It appeared shortly after pregnancy. Now I'm proud of it."

"Having Zachary is a big help," said Mary wistfully. "I can't feel the same as you."

"God will find a way in due time," said Elizabeth. "It's His baby."

"I dread the thought of going back to Nazareth," said Mary. "I dream of being stoned to death." She was visibly disturbed.

"But Rabban Hammasiah said you'd have the best care at the Temple. He doesn't want you to return to Nazareth. Remember?"

"Forgive me, Cousin," said Mary fearfully, "but thoughts contrary to the Rabban's plans keep running through my mind, especially when I am alone at night and in the early waking hours. Am I wrong to have them?"

"It's never wrong to meditate on God's will," said Elizabeth.

"It's hard to get at sometimes."

"You and your son have your mountain to climb; I have mine. Each person has his own. Tomorrow Rabban Ham-

masiah is to tell you more about your mountain—you have
your appointment with him.''

"Mary, have you heard from Joseph?" asked Rabban Hammasiah, as he escorted Zachary and his pregnant fifteen-year-old cousin from Galilee into his austere office.

"We received a note from Joseph about Papa's death," replied Mary.

"Anything more?" asked the Rabban.

"A note from Mama and Joseph," continued Mary, "asking when I planned to return to Nazareth."

"What was your reply?" asked Hammasiah.

"I answered them," intervened Zachary with his stylus and wax, "saying 'We don't know when.' " Cousin Zachary sat in a comfortable chair at a discreet distance from the Rabban's chair and his couch where Mary was receiving her admonitions. However, he was listening and ever ready to intervene in defense of the young mother.

"We deem it unnecessary for you to correspond with Joseph," advised Hammasiah in his most sonorous tones.

Again Zachary came forth, writing on his wax tablet: "No harm in an engaged couple writing to each other. Why forbid them?"

"You don't understand, Zachary," cautioned the Rabban. "The last time Mary was here, it was decided that she should reside at the Temple where she would be taken care of in better fashion than at Nazareth. She now belongs to Israel, not to any one man." The great teacher was not accustomed to being challenged by subordinates—or anyone for that matter. He was now envisioning himself as an oracle atop Mount Horeb. "To continue your affianced relationship with Joseph would cast undue suspicion upon your avowed virginity and the paternity of your child. I don't think Yahweh would approve."

"No harm," wrote Zachary. "We all attest she is already with child."

"It remains to be seen," said Hammasiah, putting his fingers to his lips as though motioning for silence. He looked piercingly at Mary, her eyes closed. She looked so tender and innocent. How naive she seemed to this man of the world. Truly a product of a small town, he thought, and of all the backward places in the nation, hers is Galilee. How easily one could mislead this young thing, so delicate a child herself. He kept tapping his lips with his fingertips as his mood suddenly changed. Imagine being contradicted by such a one as Zachary, who has been censured by heaven itself. Finally he spoke aloud in controlled tones: "Man must strive to fashion the environment in which God works best to accomplish His ordained purposes. Remember, it is man who offers the sacrifice, not God. Thus, Abraham, our father, was called to offer his own son." He then looked directly at Mary, "—Even as you now are called to offer your Joseph."

"If I do not return to Nazareth," said Mary, "Joseph will come to Jerusalem."

"Not when he finds out you are with child," said Hammasiah. "In any case, you will be in the Temple, and the authorities are prepared to protect you."

Zachary walked up to the table and placed his tablet before the Rabban: "How much time before she is incarcerated?" The last word was underlined.

"Zachary," spouted Hammasiah, "I don't like your sarcasm."

"And I don't like the games you're playing," scribbled

Zachary.

"Mary," said the Rabban, turning away from Zachary, "there will be a most convenient place for you at the Temple in three weeks. You shall be attended with the best."

All three were now standing, having taken the cue from Rabban, who rose first. No one seemed to have anything more to say—at least not aloud. The air was charged with a feeling of mutual dissatisfaction, especially between the two priests. The master of the house led his charges to the massive front door, then closed it behind them.

Zachary and Mary walked slowly down the street toward the Temple where they were to rendezvous with Aaron for the return to Ain Karim.

Mary broke the silence. "Rabban, I'm afraid of that man!"

"You have a right to be," wrote Zachary. Then he reached for her hand and held it tenderly in both of his before they again started walking toward the Temple.

* * * * * * *

The carriage with its three pensive passengers trundled along on the cobblestoned highway washed clean by the rains of yesterday. They could see far into the hills through the clear, refreshing atmosphere. The early afternoon sun was high above the western horizon, drawing shafts of prismic colors from the distant Mediterranean. The highlands were majestic today, but Mary felt more like she was adrift in the Dead Sea.

Zachary had taken note of the bundles tied inside and outside of the carriage and had commented how generous was his remuneration from the Temple this week. The Law stated that a priest should be given his portion whether he functioned or not.

It is never surprising to see Roman soldiers on highways in any part of Palestine. Today, however, there seemed to be an unusual number, and they were in a state of excitement. Occasionally one would gallop by spreading alarm. Some were dismounted and searching the rocky roadside.

"Those parade uniforms wouldn't be out there," whispered Aaron, "unless it was something serious. Vitellius must have reported activity in this area, probably a Zealot's hideout—Oh, I think we're going to be stopped."

One of the soldiers grabbed the bridle and halted the carriage; another came alongside. "Where are you going?" he asked.

"Home to Ain Karim," replied Aaron.

"Where have you been?"

"Jerusalem, at the Temple. We are priests."

"The young lady too?"

"She is a cousin, visiting from Nazareth."

The soldier walked around the carriage, poking the bags, opening some; "Did you buy all this?" he asked.

"No, it's the priest's share from the Temple," answered Aaron.

The inspection was over, and the soldier walked by Mary and gave her a smile. "You may pass," he said, which made everyone smile.

Another mile up the main road and Aaron turned off into a narrow lane leading to Zachary's home. The air was charged with expectation. Suddenly there it was—a figure of a man staggered out in front of the horses. Aaron pulled up the reins, the horses reared, and the man fell prone alongside the carriage. In a moment all three stood over him, Mary wiping the blood from his neck and side of his face. Zachary was motioning Aaron to turm him over so that they could carry him into the carriage. Then Mary cried out, "My dear God, it's Tobie!"

"He's bleeding badly," said Aaron.

"His clothes are half torn from his body," said Mary.

"You know him?" asked Aaron as he and Zachary lifted him into the crammed back seat.

"Yes," said Mary. "I'll climb in with him to check the bleeding—he has a deep gash across the base of his neck at the shoulder. Hurry, Aaron—are the soldiers coming?"

* * * * * * *

The following morning, not unlike Moses, Zachary brought with him to the breakfast table two tablets on which he had written a message for Mary. Since Elizabeth was there and had been privy to it the night before at bedtime, she read it aloud: "Rabban Hammasiah," writes Zachary, "is no longer to be trusted. He has sold out to the Sadducees for political gain. His directions given yesterday shall not be followed. The will of God is not with Hammasiah. He is now committed to Rome. He is pledged to serve Herod, who continues to murder his offspring, the seventh yesterday, in the Palace pool in Jericho. He doesn't believe any longer in the Messiah. How can he protect Him? His directions for Mary to live at the Temple are given so that the Temple authorities and Herod can keep close watch over Mary's claims of being the mother of Jesus, the Messiah. Herod will no more respect her son than he does his own. He will murder anyone who offers a threat to his throne."

"Mary," added Elizabeth, "this man is betraying Israel. Your son is an integral part of Judaism, long expected by every good Jew."

"Everyone but Rabban Hammasiah," said Mary.

Zachary reached over, picked up the tablets and rubbed out his writings. It was apparent that what he was saying should go no further.

"It seems," said Elizabeth, "that in spite of many girls who are pregnant and claiming to be objects of the ancient prophecies, your claim has warranted the attention of the Temple."

"Israel has but one God," wrote Zachary. "Today, the Temple has many. Rank needs proof, but the simpler folk have something better—faith."

"Hammasiah made a mistake in setting Joseph aside," remarked Mary. "I believe God wanted Joseph and me to be solemnly engaged for a very good reason—which is not plain to me yet...."

"Only Joseph can keep you from being stoned," said Elizabeth, "and he will give your child a name."

"But why does everybody say that he will reject me?"

"It will be a shock to him to know that you are with child and that he was not the father," added Elizabeth. "God will provide."

"At this point," wrote Zachary, "I'm not sure you're going back to Joseph. How about the young shepherd from Bethlehem who was sent to us by God yesterday? He has become an essential part of your life since you left Nazareth.''

Like a javelin striking an earthen jar, Darion came into the room declaring excitedly that the last spring moth had invaded the vineyard. ''Those oversexed maniacs are laying eggs by the thousands! All hands are needed to stamp out the enemy.'' Darion stood tall, a dark, handsome Greek, broad across the shoulders and slim around the waist.

Hand-picking moths was a crude way to save a vineyard, but, as Darion said, ''For every one you catch, you destroy a hundred skeletal caterpillars.'' Most of the household spent the greater part of that night destroying the vicious Asian Skeletonizer, so called because it ate out the soft, new leaf, leaving only the ribs in clawlike form. By the time new leaves grew, the days of sunshine would be limited, and the harvest would be diminished in size and quantity.

* * * * * * *

This was the third day the morning sun beamed through the small window to brighten the sick room where Tobie lay unconscious; however, for him it was still a world of darkness. Zachary's household was concerned for his life. Since the room was adjacent to Mary's, she kept vigil day and night, but mostly it was just listening, hoping to hear the sound of his voice.

It happened at about noon that third day. She thought she heard him say something. She ran to the room. ''Tobie, this is Mary, Mary from Galilee. You are safe. You're at my Cousin Zachary's.''

''Mary,'' he responded, and it was all he could say. His neck and shoulder were bound with linen steeped in oil and a special tea from medicinal herbs. It was obvious he had lost much blood.

''You are very much alive,'' said Mary, ''and you'd better stay that way.''

After a long moment, Tobie mumbled, ''I must be in heaven—you're here!...How long have I been here?''

''Three days.''

''I must get up,'' said Tobie, making an effort to do so.

''No! No!'' insisted Mary, pushing him back on the

pillow. "Lie still. Don't move. I'll bring you some broth."

Hearing voices in the sick room, Elizabeth and Zachary came in to help as Mary dashed through the doorway. They stood by.

"Now, here, Tobie, sip this," urged Mary. She had come back almost instantaneously, but Tobie didn't sip. He had fallen back into unconsciousness. "How is he ever going to regain his strength?" she sighed, dropping down into the chair by the bed.

This night found the thread of life stretched very thin for the shepherd boy from Bethlehem. Mary sat beside him, and when the hour of darkness fell upon Ain Karim and their room, she began her night prayer, more intensely than she ever before remembered. She was pleading with her God, reciting the Shema Israel, acknowledging Him to be the One and Only God, when she was startled out of her skin by shouts of horsemen and the clang of armor coming from the front entrance.

She heard the voice of Elizabeth saying, "You don't have to break down the doors to gain access! Please come in."

"My orders are to search this house and arrest the rebel who has been given shelter here, madam," declared the captain of the detachment.

"There is a young man here who is dying," offered Elizabeth. "We do not know his quarrel with you or the Romans. I'll take you to him."

Elizabeth was soon joined by Zachary, and Aaron, and others of the household as they headed for the sick room. Elizabeth escorted the captain into the room. Mary had lighted the lamps brightly for all to see how bad Tobie looked. "Sir," she said, "he is dying." Tobie did look bad, and he sounded like he was gasping his last.

"This is our man," stated the captain, "but we won't move him tonight. I am ordering a guard to stand watch over this house until further notice." He turned and left.

Fear like molten lava crept into every room and heart of the household and then solidified into a cold dread. God's awesome presence in the miracle of two women bearing His pregnancies, together with the loss of speech for the head of the family, tested their religious convictions daily. Rabban Hammasiah's conspiracy with the Temple authorities to trap the mother of Jesus caused many a sleepless night for Zachary and Elizabeth, prompting them to think of sending Mary back to Nazareth, yet they were fearful she might be stoned. Now, tonight, fear struck from another source. King Herod's guards could burn and sack not only the home, but the lives of all within it in less time than it had taken him to execute his own wife and sons. But fear when solidified can be a unifying principle.

"One prisoner has made prisoners of us all," said Mary as she returned to her room that evening. She had left Aaron to watch over Tobie; she was completely exhausted. She threw herself down across the bed, clothes and all, too tired even for the evening Shema Israel. "Either I have praised you all this day, Yahweh, or else you'll have to look for praises elsewhere."

Extreme tiredness robs the human will of its power with the result that the imagination goes wild and passions become more testy. Lower nature seeks supremacy. She screamed when her vivid imagination depicted a scene in which Cousin Zachary's carriage ran off the road and struck a huge boulder and overturned. She knew she wasn't dreaming. "But Ebal is dead," she said aloud. "The driver was King David, and he too is dead."

Over two months had passed since Gabriel's visit, and her girlish dreams of motherhood in the shadow of the royal throne of David now haunted her like a cruel falsehood. "Mama and Papa didn't know what to do with their little daughter," she recalled. "I was only fifteen, unwed, and they were afraid the villagers would find out. My cousin priest and his troubled wife have had nothing more than misfortune since my arrival, and I have no direction for the future."

Does a mother make the child? Is it the child that makes the mother? Who is begotten and who is begetting? This was the night for Satan. Mary was far from home, alone, and her fortress was in flames. Was something being destroyed that would give way to more of evil and less of good?

"Did someone knock?" she asked as she stared at the

door. "Come in."

"I have come to help you," spoke the voice of a woman.

"Who are you?" asked Mary.

"I am the royal midwife; I have come to deliver your baby."

"Oh, no!" cried Mary. "He is only two months old."

"But your worries will all be over, if you wish," continued the kindly voice.

"Gabriel said to me, 'The Lord be with you,' " Mary recalled. "And you are not the Lord" (Lk. 1:29).

In a moment, it was the voice of a man that spoke up. "Any time I can do anything for you, please call on me."

"A familiar voice," said Mary. "Who are you?"

"I am not here to judge you," the voice continued, "but I think I can help you."

"Judge?" she questioned. "Your voice is noble and distinct! You are a Roman."

"A poor judge, but a good Roman," he said.

"Vitellius! Thank you, God!" and Mary buried her face in her pillow wet with tears.

Chapter 15

"A plush doghouse for a lazy hound!" mused Vitellius as he began to disrobe after a boring day of inane pretensions in the halls of Herod's palace. He was supposed to be pursuing Zealots, but since the trial of the Shechem Six, he had lost interest. Rationalizing his position, he recalled his Senator father's parting words: "Enjoy Palestine! Live it up, and get some experience."

"You have a message, here, Sir," said Bartolus his servant, handing him the dainty scroll.

Vitellius perked up when he saw the tiny ribbon of blue. Suspecting it was from a female, he sniffed in an exaggerated manner. "Look, Bartolus, it has the seal of the Temple priest."

"A female priest?" said his servant. "Can't be."

"Probably an aromatic male?" said Vitellius. "Let's see."
He began to read...

> *My Dear Vitellius,*
>
> *You once very graciously said to me that if there was anything you could ever do for me, I should*

not hesitate to call on you. My need is great now.
Needless to say, it would be indiscreet to put it
in writing, and so I beg your kindness to return
to the home of Zachary in my behalf, as soon as
your busy schedule permits.

   Awaiting your word, but especially awaiting
your presence, I am,

                    Mary of Galilee.

While Vitellius read, his servant had removed his boots,
put away his paraphernalia and cloak, and was now serving him the usual five o'clock goblet of wine mixed with
jasmine and thyme, a potion prescribed for relaxation. "I
wonder what's on the young lady's mind," he pondered
aloud.

"If she is a young lady, Sir," said Bartolus, his usually
quiet aide, "it must be rather a matter of the heart. It must
not be denied."

"She is indeed a young lady, Bartolus," said Vitellius,
setting down his goblet, "but she attracts not with perfumes,
jewels, or position, but with a tenderness I've never seen
in all the Empire."

"Master, you've never spoken in this manner ever
before," said Bartolus. "Swim carefully, the net is out."

"True love, Bartolus, comes into being only with
reciprocity. Without a mutual exchange of respect and devotion, any relationship soon dies. It might continue only as
slavery."

"Slavery is not uncommon in our day, Sir."

"I would want her only as a free woman, nothing else."

"Perhaps her message has brought hope," comforted
Bartolus.

"In any case I intend to answer her personally with a
visit."

"Well spoken, Sir. Like the true Roman nobleman you
are."

Vitellius grasped the goblet with both hands and savage-
ly downed its contents into a hungry, frustrated inner being which even he didn't recognize. He felt challenged but

didn't know exactly by what.

"Are you dressing for dinner?" asked Bartolus.

"Yes, bring out the best," snapped Vitellius. "The Idumean king will have his related and unrelated concubines present, and this Roman rooster shall crow to his bevy tonight."

* * * * * * *

In the midst of the ever-moving rays of sunshine stepping over the ridge near Zachary's home, there came a lonely horseman dressed in regal finery, riding a stallion who measured his gait with a sharp, mechanical step. It was early morning, and he seemed to be in no hurry, admiring the countryside.

The Herodian guards in front of Zachary's house seemed discordant with the peaceful atmosphere, and as Vitellius dismounted, he asked, jocularly, "Has the King of Palestine taken residence here?"

"This house is under arrest, Sir," replied one of the guards, as he immediately stood in attention at the rank of the horseman.

"Who gave the order?" asked Vitellius.

"Kissufim, Captain of the palace guard, Sir."

"How long has this been going on?" asked Vitellius.

"This is the third day, Sir."

As Vitellius was about to knock on the door, Aaron opened it and welcomed him into the reception room. After a brief conversation about the situation, Aaron led Vitellius to the table in the patio. There was no need to summon Mary, for she was waiting, keeping a daily vigil with prayer.

"Vitellius!" cried Mary hastening from her room. "How good of you to come."

"Didn't think I'd have the pleasure of seeing you so soon," said Vitellius. "Coming to Rome with me?" he teased.

"Herod's guards won't allow it," smiled Mary. "But, Vitellius, please come into the dining room; you're probably without breakfast."

"Try again. I'm hungry, but not for food."

"Vitellius, we are in trouble," pleaded Mary as they entered.

"Tell me about it."

Vitellius was served a hearty breakfast, and between his gulps, Mary gave him the whole story of how they found Tobias the shepherd boy from Bethlehem and were nursing him back to life.

"He must be important," said the Roman, "or Herod wouldn't bother with a house arrest."

"He's very young, and only a shepherd," reasoned Mary mildly.

"Probably a very good recruiter."

"Will you help?"

"If they were Roman soldiers, I'd take them with me when I leave, but palace guards are like marble columns—once in place, they're hard to move. . . . I'll do something—please don't worry."

As if they were eavesdropping, and it seems they were, in came Aaron, Elizabeth, and Zachary, greeting Vitellius like a long-lost relative. The young Roman knew the desired meeting with Mary was over; now the shaloms of courteous hospitality would bore him. He rose not only to greet Mary's relatives, but even more to take his leave.

* * * * * * *

Zachary came hurrying down the pathway through the vineyard and into the courtyard, fingering a small object close to his eyes, as though it were an injured butterfly. Mary hurried to meet him. Unable to speak, he gestured to her to take it; it was for her. Mary took the little quill, opened it and read on the tiny bit of split parchment: *"Mother needs you. I need you. Come home—or I'm coming to get you! Love, Joseph."*

"Joseph wouldn't say that if he knew I was pregnant," said Mary. "Would anyone in Nazareth want me?"

Zachary kept nodding his head in the affirmative, although it was more out of sympathy than conviction. From the large sleeve of his robe, he drew the ever present pad and stylus and wrote: "Say nothing about this to Hammasiah. Remember you have an appointment with him the day after tomorrow."

"Somehow I dread it." said Mary. "Are you coming with

me, Rabban?''

"An absolute no!'' indicated Zachary, pointing his thumbs down and shaking his head back and forth with indignation.

"Oh, don't abandon me now,'' begged Mary. "I have already lost all my dear ones.''

They both sat at once when they came to the patio table, and Zachary scribbled along on his pad, as she peered over his shoulder. "Hammasiah is not the man he once was when he was hungry. Today he is a victim of forces beyond his control. He has succumbed to the Sadducees, is more a Roman than a Jew, is a pragmatist with King Herod—and frankly I doubt whether he any longer believes in a Messiah.''

"Rabban, this means he doesn't believe my story. He never did?''

"The Temple authorities are not convinced that your Messiah, or anyone else's, shall limit himself to a spiritual kingdom. If Herod felt that a young girl was carrying the unborn 'son of the Most High, and the Lord will give him the throne of his father David—and he will reign over the house of Jacob forever'—as you told me the Angel Gabriel proclaimed to you (Lk. 1:32), he would issue an order to have every pregnant girl in Israel aborted, even if it meant the death of the mother. He has done even more hideous things.''

"God will not permit His Jesus to be aborted. What must I do?''

"Aaron will go with you to Rabban's, and you must not divulge your feelings or fears. I'm afraid I might show mine.''

"Rabban Hammasiah is playing games with God. He— he can't win.''

"Cousin Mary,'' Zachary continued, "you are free, *free!''*

"Free? Free to do what?'' she asked.

"Freedom is the cry of the anarchist when one doesn't know what to do with freedom. It is sweet contentment when one has purpose like you have. Yours is but one single-minded task—give birth to your baby.''

"When the bird is freed, it flies,'' said Mary quoting the

Psalmist. "I have escaped the Temple's influence like a bird from the hunter's net (Ps. 124:7). But I have already flown once—to come here...."

"Alexander flies both ways."

"You two have been gesticulating," interrupted Elizabeth, "like twin willows in a dreadful khamsin. Here, try some of this," she offered as she set down an earthen jug of honeyed wine.

"It's more than a dreadful khamsin," said Mary.

"Yes, I know all about it," replied Elizabeth. "If one is to become God's wheat, Mary, one must first be ground by the teeth of beasts and made pure." She poured the purplish wine.

"Rabban Hammasiah seemed so kind at first," lamented Mary.

"He has a part to play in your life," wrote Zachary, "but we have not yet discerned it. Freedom comes first; direction moves a step at a time."

"M-a-r-y!" came the moaning cry from the sick room. "M-a-r-y...."

"It's Tobie!" Mary jumped. "Could this be step number one?"

"Don't let the guards hear him," urged Elizabeth.

Mary rushed into Tobie's room: "I'm here, Tobie!" she said reassuringly. "Talk to me softly. I hear you well." She wiped his face and held his hand in both of hers.

Zachary entered the room with the jar of honeyed wine. It was still warm. He gave Tobie a long stiff drink, the first nourishment in six days. The patient brightened. His eyes were alive. "How did I get here?" he asked.

"This is my cousin, Zachary, Tobie," said Mary. "We are at Ain Karim. We found you on the back road bleeding to death and brought you here."

"Did you find any of the others?" asked Tobie.

"No one else," said Mary.

"There were eight recruits," said Tobie, attempting to sit up.

"You mean you were recruiting for the Zealots?" asked Mary.

"No—I was searching for you," said Tobie with a smile.

"Well, at least you found me."

Zachary had left the room but reappeared with Eliabeth, who came carrying a bowl of broth from Cassandra's kitchen. "Things sound normal in here," said Elizabeth. "One must be in good physical condition to disagree. Here, take this broth, Tobias—it's just for you."

"I was on my way to Jerusalem with eight recruits," said Tobie between gulps, "but obviously we didn't make it. Judas and Sadduk are there. They must be notified. They are preparing big things against the establishment. They need men."

"Isn't there a better way of promoting the cause of Israel?" Mary drew up a chair.

"You got your answer in the headquarters at Mt. Ebal, Mary," said Tobie. "The Romans will get theirs in Jerusalem. The masses are joining the Zealots everywhere. Some of the wealthy Sadducees are supporting their cause."

"Tobie, I wish you would find a more peaceful way to restore Judaism. Your present tactics are inviting the Roman legions. It's suicide."

"You discount the supernatural element, my dear," said Tobie. "The Zealots know that the Messiah will come and restore the kingdom. We are making straight his paths."

"It won't be done by force," said Mary. "This Kingdom shall be a voluntary one based on love."

"Enough idealism from you two," intervened Elizabeth.

"The spirit is restored by righteous anger," wrote Zachary.

Tobie began to show his tiredness. He just stared at the broth—like he was going to fall asleep with his eyes wide open.

Aaron, who had been looking for the master, slipped into the room.

"You're right on time, Aaron," said Mary. "Would you offer a prayer of thanks for Tobie's recovery?"

After he finished, he turned to Zachary and whispered, "Rabban, the sentries have left the premises. We are no longer under arrest."

Mary heard the good news. "Another prayer of thanks, Aaron. This time for Vitellius."

Chapter 16

An expert midwife was seen entering the home of Zachary on this glorious day in June. Grapevines whistled in the wind, and the pigeons were restless with expectation. Yona was her name, and she came none too soon from the neighboring village of Shemesh. Elizabeth's time had come.

Mary's education now began. Yona usually did not permit anyone "to get in the way" as she worked, but having been informed that Mary was pregnant, she welcomed the oppportunity to be helpful.

Meanwhile, and often these days, Zachary was communing with the Deity seeking guidance for his wife and cousin, both looking to him for answers. He faltered occasionally under the nagging censure of silence, but it gave him more insight into the problems of others for he related to them mostly by listening. He now listened to God in his chapel. He could feel a change coming over him; the shameful inadequacy of manhood that haunted him in the past was now becoming a heartfelt feeling of fatherhood in the present. He waited for the Lord to speak but had his ear attuned to the direction of Yona in the delivery room.

"Call me, Lord, I am ready to serve!" he prayed.

As so often happens, the Lord spoke through another. "Come, Zachary," shouted Yona. "You have a son!"

Everyone came. The courtyard filled with people—Aaron, his family—Darion, his family. The pigeons came, flew low, and tumbled. Zachary hesitated at the door, knowing the tradition of ancient Israel that forbade the father to enter the delivery room before the birth was completed. There was good reason for this, for too many men interfered with the rhythm of childbirth by attempting to take over at the crucial time.

When Yona was about to present Zachary with his newborn son, Aaron placed a chair in the doorway from which the new father would pontificate. He announced, *"For our sakes a child is born; to our race a son is given"* (Is. 9:5).

Zachary then held his son proudly on his knees, thus officially recognizing him to be his legitimate son.

"Bekor?" cried Darion in Hebrew. "His firstborn!"

"Bekor! Bekor!" echoed and reechoed the household, uniting their voices with a few visiting friends.

"In behalf of our Rabban Zachary," spoke Aaron the Levite, "I have been asked to tell you that his firstborn son shall be named and circumcised eight days hence, it being the day before the vigil of the Sabbath. You are all invited to the festivities."

Bursts of joy and jubilation filled the courtyard, sending vibrations down the Sorek River Valley and over the ridge to Jerusalem. It was to the Temple and his fellow priests that Zachary wanted the news to spread. It did.

Meanwhile in the delivery room, Elizabeth, somewhat shaken up by the experience, was being comforted by Yona and Mary. She said courageously, "The Lord's work is done; I paid willingly."

Mary observed every last detail. She was especially attracted to the birthstool Yona had brought with her. It was crude but practical, she noticed, having an extra strong backrest at a comfortable angle with the floor, and the horseshoe shaped chair was little higher than a conventional chair. There were extensions upon which the mother could brace her feet, which kept her knees slightly bent so as to assist in parturition.

"It really helps," said Yona, noticing Mary's intensity. "In Elizabeth's case it was a necessity, for others it is a luxury."

"I doubt whether one so young as you," said Elizabeth, "will have any use for it."

"I should take my business to Egypt," remarked Yona as she began to scrub the stool. "Women there have great difficulty in delivery, but our Jewish women, well, they just drop their babies anywhere and are ready to go back to work the next day. They brag about not needing such a one as me."

"If you're not needed, Yona, and the man is not permitted in the room," asked Mary, "who is there to assist?"

"No one! The mother is on her own. However, usually there is someone around for the first baby."

All present had seen Zachary's baby, and he now returned it to Yona, who rubbed it with salt and swaddled it. After much wailing and crying, the baby became quiet and was placed next to its mother.

"Notice, Yona," said Mary, "a mucus keeps running out of his mouth. Is he ill?"

"Not at all, he is just expelling what he swallowed being born. It won't last more than a day."

"Why does he keep looking at me?" asked Mary. "He seems to want something."

"He really sees nothing the first few days, no matter how he looks," answered Yona with practiced patience. "Right now all he needs is warmth to help him adjust to the world outside the womb. Tomorrow, he'll take a little water, and in about three days he'll find his mother's breast and know for himself what to do."

Elizabeth took it all in, her face flushed after exertion, but beaming and youthful. In giving life, she gained some for herself. She never felt so important and useful as today.

"I'll stop by in a few days, Elizabeth," said Yona. "Meanwhile, let nature take its course, don't force anything."

"You've been just wonderful! Thanks, Yona."

A heavenly stillness descended upon the room and its inhabitants, and the only sound heard was a newly-born son sucking his thumb, an action learned in prenatal life. Even his position in sleep was not new, for he had taken it many times while resting in the womb, his arms and legs curled up, the back bowed and his head on his chest.

"He's had a hard day," said Elizabeth to Mary.

"So has his mother. Are you sleepy?"

"No, but I would like a cup of wine with a dash of water, please."

"Was the experience very painful, Cousin?" asked Mary as she poured the mixture.

"Pain is a messenger. It tells you something," said Elizabeth deliberately. "As the frequency and intensity of the pain increased, the good news was that my baby was ever closer to being born. Too much pain is difficult to endure, but no pain at all would break down communication with the little person coming into the world. Severe pain gives us the signal that there is something wrong and needs attention."

"It must give you a good feeling all over to think that you brought forth a new life, a new person."

"Elation is mixed with pain," continued Elizabeth, "and when delivery is finished, the elation continues. I feel only elation now, a pervading joy."

"You are very brave, Cousin."

"I only appeared brave, perhaps," commented Elizabeth. "I was afraid; I thought something old like me would break. When he gave me the most pain, I returned his greeting with an extra push toward the breach. It helped both of us. Are you afraid, Mary?"

"Not really. I ask God to allow all of it to the fullest measure."

"The thing to remember is: Don't hurry it. You'll be surprised at how quickly and easy it goes when you let up to rest both yourself and the little one."

"The intimate relationship between mother and baby starts early in life, doesn't it?" said Mary

"It may be he initiates it with his first kick." They both laughed.

"Did you worry about anything?"

" 'Is he all there?' I asked Yona. When she assured me, I then relaxed and let elation set it."

"I remember," said Mary. "But, Cousin Elizabeth, I've been asking too many questions. You must be tired."

"Oh, no. This is very relaxing. It has a quality of an after-show, if I may be allowed to be funny."

"You may be funny, if you permit me to be a first grader." Mary hoped Elizabeth would continue telling about the experience. "One other thing troubles me," continued Mary. "Surely you remember the words of Yahweh as recorded in Genesis: 'I will multiply your pains in childbearing; you shall give birth to your children in pain...' (Gn. 3:16)."

"I don't look upon it so much as punishment," said Elizabeth, "although it was so intended, but I think of it as a part and parcel of the process. I really think some women would feel cheated if they didn't have it at all."

"Maybe, but, Cousin, I'm thinking of the next two lines: 'Your yearning shall be for your husband, yet he will lord it over you.' I know not a man, and who is my husband?"

"Do you want to be a mother, or a martyr?" asked Elizabeth with a smile.

"A mother, of course, but if I don't have a husband, I may wind up being the kind of martyr not even God would want."

"The Father of your child will see to it that that doesn't happen," assured Elizabeth. "Try not to anticipate God's actions, my dear girl; bear in mind that all things work out well for those who love God (cf. Ro. 8:28). If Zachary shows great concern about me and his son, needless to say the Holy Spirit who overshadowed you will show even greater concern. Live by this trust."

But willingness to serve is not enough to continue serving. Elizabeth's energy was running low, and her efforts to bolster the cause of the young mother of Jesus began to wane. Her eyelids became heavy. Mary was on the lookout for these symptoms. As soon as they appeared, she excused herself.

"I've been to school," she mused as she crossed the courtyard to her room. "What a beautiful woman I've seen!"

* * * * * * *

Light all the candles. Place lighted incense in every thurible. Sing all the psalms of praise. Old man Zachary has been vindicated. "I have fathered a son!" repeated Zachary to himself as he walked to and fro and all around his little chapel that night. He couldn't sleep. Who wanted to sleep when he could stay awake and think about his son?

The thought of his son evoked the thought of God's messenger, Gabriel, and somehow Zachary always finished his soliloquies by pleading for forgiveness:

> *Forgive me messenger of God!*
> *I had no right to doubt you.*
> *Suffices the long rod*
> *applied in silence*
> *that lasted nine months!*
> *It was more human frailty*
> *than the word of a priest,*
> *childless to say the least,*
> *who lost respect among*
> *his virile colleagues.*
> *Forgive me, messenger of God!*
> *The son is born—I am his father!*

Only a man who is truly superior can be genuinely humble. Tonight Zachary was superior; he felt his manhood and was willing to humble himself before the messenger as well as his message—a little late, but at least now. His son would give him stature at the Temple, so now he had bargaining gems with the angels of heaven and promised a total commitment to his work, if only his voice would be returned. He visualized himself dealing with confidence and authority with Temple people, happier to serve. With some, he thought, his words would bounce off the Temple walls and rattle their souls, and they would eat the thistles of uncharitableness they had sown not too long ago. No more would they say, "Sterile Zachary and his frigid wife!"

But tonight, though his thoughts were strong, his voice was not yet to be heard.

Chapter 17

Tobie's healing wounds, like withering bands of goat skin, pulled his head toward the left shoulder. He strained to move the cluster of pale, slender fingers protruding from a sling. "Look, Mary," he exulted, "I can move my fingers."

"New flesh needs exercising and oil," she advised. "We'll continue our treatments after breakfast. In time your scar tissue will be as supple as a little lamb's nose. I'm afraid you'll live to fight again."

"Only you could deserve that kind of cure," he said dejectedly.

"What's wrong with being a good shepherd and raising sheep for Romans *and* Zealots?"

"For Romans only, if they promise to eat the lambs in Rome."

"And how about you? When do you plan on eating lamb in Bethlehem?" asked Mary.

"What's more important is, when are you going to eat lamb in the Temple? I heard that Rabban Hammasiah has set a date."

"I haven't heard from Cousin Zachary yet," replied Mary. "He will tell me how this is to be accomplished. What are your plans?"

"I'm indebted to Zachary," said Tobie. "I plan to stay here until my debt is paid. I can work with one arm for a while, and then with both as long as it is necessary. But, Mary—how will I ever repay you? Will you permit me to see you at the Temple?"

"You paid me in advance, and if all you did for me and Deborrah were placed on the balance scales, I think I would be the one found wanting."

"Not so, but thanks. You know, Mary, when my arm heals I would like to settle down in a home of my own in Bethlehem and take care of you and your child. . . . I've been thinking—"

"Please don't, Tobie. Sure, there's no harm in saying what you're thinking, but it's preposterous to think that you could bring a pregnant girl to your home town—to your family—and expect them to accept me."

"I've been waiting to ask you, and now I did. Remember that I did, if ever that time comes when Bethlehem figures in your plans."

"What you said was a nice thing," said Mary. "Thanks, Tobie."

"No doubt you have your heart set on Joseph and Nazareth." He didn't seem to want to let go of the subject. "I envy him."

"What makes you think that Joseph and Nazareth will accept me anymore than you and Bethlehem? Right now my heart is feeding my baby, and I have placed myself completely in the hands of Zachary and will abide by his decisions."

"You won't make it without a husband, not in our Judaistic traditions," offered Tobie.

"God will provide," said Mary.

"You make God a responsible person," he objected.

"That he is!" said Mary. "He has a plan for every person."

"What's my plan?" he asked lightly.

"Right now, it's for you to carry *your* 'baby' in your *sling,* calmly and patiently. If you do, you'll be surprised how much God can teach you."

"My baby!" said Tobie, swinging his left arm with his right. "I've just named it 'Mary'."

* * * * * * *

Zachary the father, vested in the colorful regalia of his priestly office, following the tradition of his forefathers, gently handling a flint-knife, straightway cut off the foreskin of his eight-day-old son. The terrified child let out a cry of fright and pain, while the innocent blood flowed freely. Aaron immediately handed Zachary a paste made of oil, wine, and cumin, which he placed solidly about the wound, and then bandaged it with a stripping of clean white cloth. When finished, he gave the crying infant to his sympathetic and comforting mother.

The sacred rite, marking the reception of the offspring into the Zachary clan, was performed in the open, before members of the household and friends. The Jew believed that circumcision was originated by God himself, on the occasion when he directed Abraham to perform it for all his descendants (Gn. 17:10). It was never omitted and always called for great celebration. The worst thing a Jew could call anyone was "uncircumcised." It was a fighting word.

Elizabeth loved her baby and immediately offered him his usual morning fare at her breast. Momentarily he forgot his wound and was fast at work, stopping only for a deep sigh or a short cry.

Relatives and friends gathered around mother and child, now seated in the center of the courtyard in a large chair. Mary watched Elizabeth's every move in wonderment and admiration. Would her son bring her as much joy and prestige? Would there be someone present to perform the sacred rite as Zachary did? She fearfully recalled how Zipporah, the wife of Moses, did it herself for her own son, and thus saved her husband's life before God (Ex. 4:25).

Cousin Marta, having come from the mountainous region of Samaria, approached Elizabeth, and in her usual voice asked loudly, "What are you going to name the child? We're all waiting to hear."

"Marta," cautioned Elizabeth, "you sound like you are making a public announcement. No, we haven't forgotten.

I hope you don't mind waiting."

"Have you chosen the name yet?" she asked more softly.

"His father shall name him—and very soon." Then she turned to Mary and asked her to find Aaron and Zachary and have them come to her right away.

"My dear Cousin Elizabeth—" interjected Mary, "don't look now, but here comes Rabban of the Sanhedrin. He is being escorted by Zachary and Aaron—"

"The old stinkin' goat!" said Elizabeth. "He's late and acting like he's coming to his own circumcision party."

"I'm afraid he has me on his mind," said Mary. "Our last meeting bruised his large ego."

"He seems to be upset with Zachary," said Elizabeth, raising her baby aloft.

"My most sincere congratulations, Mother Elizabeth," droned Rabban Hammasiah, bowing low and placing his hand on the infant's head in blessing. "This is your day. You have mothered a fine-looking son."

"Thank you, Sir," said Elizabeth, as she wiped some regurgitation from her baby's mouth.

The crowd pressed in around Zachary and his distinguished guest. Some had noticed the heated conversation and were sporting for more.

"Zachary, you must feel as big as Mount Hermon," intoned the Rabban looking over the crowd, "as important as Abraham giving birth to a nation." The Rabban was overdoing it intentionally. In a lesser tone, he turned to Mary and asked, "And you, my daughter, why didn't you show at the Temple for your entrance examination? I expect to see you there next week, same day, same time—"

"When are you going to name the child, Zachary," came the shrill voice of Marta. "What is his name?"

"What's your problem, Zachary?" asked the Rabban. "A child is usually named at the end of the rite of circumcision."

Zachary's face flushed. He tried to speak. He started to look for his stylus and pad.

Elizabeth explained, "He disrupted the ceremony to welcome you, Rabban."

"His name shall be his father's!" shrieked Marta. Several

guests audibly agreed with her.

"No, no," said Elizabeth. "Say it, Zachary!" she urged, momentarily forgetting he couldn't speak. "Remember, Gabriel said it."

Aaron handed Zachary the tablet. A hush fell over the crowd. Zachary wrote something, and then stepping up on the bench, he read it loud and clear: "...And you shall call his name John!"

All stood motionless, stupefied. They heard again the old priest's voice. He spoke. For a moment the name was less important.

"He shall be great," continued Zachary, *"in the sight of the Lord, and his spirit shall be that of Elijah, preparing the way of the Messiah our Savior!"* Again he said, *"And his name is John!"* (Lk. 1:67).

"Yahweh Sabbaoth," uttered Elizabeth, "my man speaks again! The days of punishment are ended. Praise God!"

Zachary stepped down from the chair into the arms of his wife, while everyone witnessed the unity of his family and recognized the will of God as they repeated, "His name is John." The presence of the Almighty was felt and accepted.

Rabban Hammasiah, pressed by the crowd's attention to Zachary, was now placed in a minor role. Already upset by Zachary's failure to bring Mary to the Temple, he now began to bully his old friend. "Your deviation from tradition in naming your son will get you into serious trouble, Zachary. The priests now have added testimony against you."

"Only if you put them up to it," said Zachary.

"What's more, your son does not deserve the name 'John'," said the Rabban, poking his finger into Zachary's face.

"And why not?" asked Zachary sternly.

"Because it means 'God abounds in grace and mercy'," growled the Rabban, "and for you to apply it to your son is blasphemy."

"My rights are not limited by one such as you," answered Zachary.

"We shall see, and very soon," barked Hammasiah.

"Your beloved little cousin, three months pregnant, is to be called before the Temple Board within the week!"

Zachary said nothing. Had he again lost his voice?

"You'll need someone like me, my friend," continued the Rabban.

"I have someone better and bigger," said Zachary.

Rabban Hammasiah turned his back on Zachary's family and headed for the front exit, bumping people in his haste.

Mary and Elizabeth stood stunned, but in an attitude of prayer. Zachary, refusing to succumb to the onslaught, took his son from Aaron's wife and lifted him heavenward toward the expansive blue sky. Then the old proud priest of the order of Abia began to chant:

"Blessed be the Lord, One is he, The God of Israel!
He has wedged himself between the enemy and his people.
Indeed he abounds in grace and mercy now, even more
than in the time of Abraham our Nation's father.
And John! You, my firstborn son, you shall do all things
right!
Prepare the way for Jesus, as Gabriel said, lead our
people to repent, guide them to peace!
Upon this house, and all within it now, God, let there
be peace!"

* * * * * * *

Happy, optimistic Yona, everybody's midwife, broke the tension of two long days of worry and planning at Zachary's home when she dropped in to check on the newly-born John; she knew his name; she said everybody in the Sorek Valley knew it. She reminded all present that her return visit was included in the initial fee.

She found John in the midst of strenuous exercise, flailing his arms, kicking at the covers, arching his back, and pursing his mouth that ran with saliva. His complexion was a healthy pink.

"Well, that's a good boy," said Yona. "Let's take a look at your wounds." She flipped back the covers and untied the wrapping. "A perfect circular scar in the making—

look," she invited Elizabeth and Mary. Then she placed a
new paste and bandage over the circumcision. The second
wound was older; all that was left was a slight bump on a
baby navel.

"The cord you tied so well, Yona," said Elizabeth, "—it
shriveled, became very black, and dropped off just the other
day. You may be interested to know that the placenta, which
you called stubborn, left no fragments, and I was clean in
a day."

"All very fine," concluded Yona. "What are John's
eating habits?"

"He had his first meal after two days, when my milk sup-
ply became established. He has a large appetite."

"How often do you feed him?"

"Four times a day—and, yes, once during the night."

"Stop the night feeding as soon as you can," advised
Yona. "How about elimination?"

"I seem to be changing him all the time. Tell me, it is
normal for him to eliminate and burp so frequently?" asked
Elizabeth.

"If he didn't, you'd have a sick baby." The midwife then
proceeded with some of her home-grown tests. She gently
touched his cheek, and he responded by turning his head
and starting a sucking motion. She declared, "Very good!"
She placed her index finger in the palm of his hand, and
waited for him to curl his tiny wrinkled fingers around it,
gripping it tightly. "Fine boy," she said.

Elizabeth was visibly pleased and smiled a nod of approval
at Mary, who was drinking it all in. Mary nodded back, saying, "My boy will do as well." They laughed.

Yona then picked up the baby and set him down on his
stomach. He began a swimming-like crawling motion. It
looked funny, and they continued their joyful spirit.

"No blemishes. Good functions. You've got yourself a
fine baby!" said Yona.

But after Yona turned John right side up, Mary noticed
that he looked cross-eyed at her. She startled, but Yona
assured her, "This happens often with the newborn. The
ability to focus one's eyes is a great achievement, and it takes
a little time for the muscles to work it out together. Give

him a few weeks."

"Yona, I would have been lost without you," said Elizabeth. "Thanks and blessings!"

"Now tell me about yourself," urged Yona.

"Nothing to report."

"Are you eating well?" asked Yona.

"Yes, but seem to be losing weight."

"Every mother should lose weight after childbirth," she observed. "It's mostly liquid, and better you get rid of it. The baby loses the first few days, too."

"Yona, do many babies fall asleep in the middle of a meal?" asked Elizabeth, tongue in cheek.

"Rest is sometimes more demanding than hunger," explained the midwife. "However, if you suspect he is forming a bad habit, remove the source of food from his mouth, and his instinct to go out and find it will quickly awaken him. But don't play games."

"Mind if I ask you a question, Yona?" asked Mary. "Some mothers have trouble with the nipple become extremely sore even to the point of bleeding. What does one do?"

"This doesn't happen to our Jewish women, but it does happen among the Egyptians. Our women prepare themselves weeks before by applying oil on their nipples, keeping them supple and exercising their erectile power. This makes for a large, soft nipple. One that is hard and dry will crack easily, as you might guess."

"Does it ever happen that a mother is unable to feed her baby?" asked Mary. "What then?"

"If a mother alternates the feeding station whenever she thinks of it and sees to it that the infant does not go on sucking after his meal, she will keep ahead of it. It's a rare thing to have to skip a meal because of this condition."

"Do you advocate feeding from mouth to mouth?" asked Elizabeth.

"Only in extreme cases," said Yona. "In time a little goat's milk, plus some sugar-water, will go a long way to tide over the rest period for the feeding stations."

Baby John missed the entire conversation. He was in his favorite position, a prenatal curl with thumb in mouth, fast asleep.

On the third day after Yona's visit, as the first rays of sunshine reflected off the stucco walls of Zachary's home, an elite patrol in bright silver breastplate and armor came riding over the eastern ridge and stationed itself at all exits.

"Welcome to the finest of the Temple guards!" greeted Zachary with outstretched arms. "What brings you to the humble abode of a Temple priest this early in the day?"

The captain dismounted. "We have orders to arrest one, Mary of Galilee, and another, a Tobias of Bethlehem."

The soldiers did not wait for the amenities, but hurriedly passed through the entrance into the courtyard. One walked directly to Mary's room. All were well instructed. The captain himself bolted to Tobie's quarters. Both rooms proved to be as empty and clean as Cassandra's washtub at bedtime. The captain ordered a continued search of the house and grounds.

The members of the household all showed resentment at the "surprise" intrusion by the soldiers and acted as speechless as their Rabban once was.

Zachary repaired to the comfort of his office, where he waited for the fuming, frustrated captain.

He finally entered without knocking. "Are you responsible for this house and its occupants?" he asked.

"Yes, except when my good wife orders me not to," replied Zachary.

"I'll take no smart answers," snorted the captain.

"Sorry, Sir."

"Where are the two culprits, Mary and her Zealot friend?" asked the impatient captain.

"Aren't you Aenas," asked Zachary softly, "the genial captain who inspects the priests' quarters? Your family comes from Lydda. Right?"

"Your memory serves you well, Sir, but I have my orders. If I'm unable to arrest Mary, then I'm to bring in the master of the house, Zachary."

"Zachary I am!"

"I'll allow you a few moments to pack your things."

"Who signed your orders?" asked Zachary.

"Gyshahim, superintendent of the Temple guards."

"Did he receive his orders from the Sanhedrin? I have an old friend there."

"It is none of my business, Sir," said the captain. "It matters only whether I bring in the prisoners."

"Prisoners? That's a harsh word, Captain." Zachary began to pack a leather saddlebag, picking up some papers and writing materials off his desk. "You know, one is not a prisoner until convicted of a crime."

"You may take warm clothes, Sir," the captain condescended.

"I have comfortable quarters at the Temple. Anyway, I'm planning on returning very soon."

"Very well, Sir."

"Now, may I say 'Shalom' to my dear wife and household?"

"Rabban!" said Aaron in the courtyard. "I can't believe it! Why must they subject you to this outrage?"

Zachary waved his arms to quiet him.

"Your colleagues will be astounded," continued Aaron, "to see you return to the Temple escorted by the elite guard."

"They will think I deserve the escort for fathering a fine, healthy son!"

Chapter 18

On the open road that followed the flat coastline of the
Mediterranean Sea, a striding camel hurried northward
carrying two passengers, a man and a girl, with a few bundles
of impedimenta. It was a light load for the strong, speedy
beast, so that instinctively he knew that haste was more important than comfort. He responded eagerly for his anxious
but patient riders, showing no sign of fatigue, thirst, or
hunger, even though it was late in the afternoon and they
had been traveling since dawn.

The two fleeing passengers were less experienced. They
could not discern whether they were more tired because they
were watching for pursuers, they were wrestling with their
worries, or they were not suited for nonstop travel on a
speeding camel's bumping back.

"At this rate, Mary," said Aaron, "We should be in Kefar
Vitkin within the light of day."

"Perhaps we should slow down," suggested Mary.
"Zachary warned us not to go in while it was daylight."

"Are you tired?"

"I could go on, but you decide what's best, Aaron."

"We'll stop and stretch our legs."

"Along the seashore?"

"No, too dangerous. Let's get beyond the cluster of bushy terebinths where we will not be seen."

Zachary had instructed Aaron to stay in Kefar Vitkin overnight with his friend, Rabbi Amman Eber, who lived there in retirement. There was no way of notifying the Rabbi of their coming, for the move from Ain Karim left no time for anything more than to get a camel and go. Anyone from Zachary's household would be welcome; no explanation would be necessary. Rabbi Amman Eber dropped in unannounced many times at Zachary's on his way to Jerusalem. They were both of the same class of priesthood, the Abia class, and had been in touch since boyhood.

The reason for the need of arriving after dark was anonymity, for fifteen miles beyond Kefar Vitkin was the new city of Caesarea, recently built by King Herod, where he kept a sizable garrison of soldiers who sometimes wandered into neighboring towns.

"We must not disturb the brood of vipers," said Aaron as they were once more on their way.

"Zachary thinks of everything. I wonder how he's faring today?"

"When we arrive at Kefar Vitkin, we will have traveled sixty miles since we last saw him. Amazing, isn't it?"

"How far do we travel tomorrow?" she asked.

"Only about thirty-five miles—the road is excellent, taking us over the plains of Esdraelon."

"I can't wait," Mary jested, flexing her back.

The camel began to walk as if he understood. His steps were softly taken and he glided along evenly, so that the casual observer wouldn't surmise he had traveled far and was tired. It takes as much grace and energy for a camel to do this as it does to stride along at high speed.

"Darion did well in getting us such good transportation," said Aaron. "He had little time."

Once the sun sets into the Mediterranean, it becomes dark quickly. Today the twilight sky was aglow with reddish hues, reflecting on the faces of the travelers and drenching the Highland to the east in a purple majesty. It was an inspiring time for meditation, as well as an omen of a sunny tomorrow.

Mary reached into the folds of her sash, Joseph's gift of long ago, and withdrew a small folded piece of parchment, the seal of which was already broken, and the message read several times since yesterday.

> *Dear Little Girl from Galilee:*
>
> *The Temple guards, under order of the Sanhedrin, will be out to arrest you before sunrise tomorrow, you, Tobias, and Zachary. You have many enemies at the Temple and at the palace, fomented by Rabban Hammasiah. They want your unborn baby. Run for it, little one! As for the men, I care not. But, you, please stay alive. You are my hope.*
>
> *The Shechem Judge.*

Mary tasted intimacy in the message, and her heart jumped a little every time she read the signature. She smothered a laugh.

"What's so funny?" asked Aaron. "Every time you read that thing you embrace yourself with a full circle smile."

"Not funny—but sweet," answered Mary, "I once pleaded for the lives of six condemned Zealots and lost; but what I didn't know was that I saved the lives of two adults and an unborn child—Jesus is still alive—I hope Tobie made it."

* * * * * * *

"Son, I'd rather have you wounded and at home than chasing Romans around the Judaean hills," said Tobie's mother as she placed some food in front of him.

"No, mother, not that," argued Tobie. "There's no honor in staying home when my country is overrun with Roman rats. Somebody has to defend our homes and our way of life, or we'll all go down the cesspool."

"Let somebody else's son do it," said his mother. "I only have you."

"You didn't used to talk like that. It must be the sight of this banged-up shoulder that's bothering you. Mary wouldn't talk like that.''

"Who in heaven's name is Mary?''

"God's angel from Galilee—the sweetest person on earth!''

"And she believes in war?''

"No, not exactly. She believes in peace and is willing to pay the price for it. Her life militates against war—she's fighting the enemy all the time—''

"What kind of weapons does she use?'' asked his mother.

"Unconventional—like love, almsgiving, doing good, being true to yourself . . . and lots more.''

"I'm glad you're home, Son! And this time you're home to stay! Women and wars will have to wait—and a long time, I hope.'' Without asking, his mother poured some more soup into Tobie's bowl.

"I'll wait, Mother, for war, yes. But for Mary? If she sent me word today that she wanted me, I'd be on my way! Tobie looked across the room with dreamy-eyed determination, and gradually things began to be fuzzy and distant. He stopped eating.

Chapter 19

"Why has the house become so small?" asked Mary as the tall, rocking camel came to a stop at the entrance. From her lofty position, she could almost see over the top of it. It looked abandoned.

"There's smoke from the chimney," observed Aaron, "and no doubt a lovely lady at home." He brought the camel to his knees, so Mary could slide off.

Quickly Mary scanned the old homestead. The olive trees hadn't all been harvested, animals ran back into the corral, frightened by the monstrous camel, pigeons swooped overhead, and weeds were in abundance everywhere.

The old wooden door opened slowly, and Anna came forth wiping her hands in her apron, with her hair falling over her face. She wasn't expecting anyone, especially a camel and two extraordinary passengers. She was in complete disarray.

"Yahweh Sabbaoth!" she exclaimed. "Why didn't you let me know? But thank God you're safe—you look fine, Mary—." Mother and daughter fell into each other's arms.

"Where is Papa?" asked Mary.

"Laid to rest beyond the pigeon rocks, where he always wanted to be," related Anna sadly. "He offered himself that you might live. Thank God you're home—and is this," she turned toward Aaron, "one of Zachary's...."

"This is Aaron, Cousin Zachary's Levite," said Mary.

"Shalom, Aaron! Won't you come inside?" invited Anna meekly. "Both the place and I miss your father, Mary. We are so inept. Joseph comes by, but he is very busy."

"Is he coming today?" asked Mary.

"No, tomorrow is his day. Now, Daughter, if you haven't forgotten that it takes wood to cook a meal," said Anna, glancing at Mary's new clothes, "fetch some, and we'll prepare a lunch for you and the young Levite. You must be hungry."

"Not so young, Mother, but very hungry," responded Aaron. "Thanks. While you're busy in here, I'll go out and feed the camel."

"Aaron can only stay over night, Mama," said Mary, dropping the wood next to the hearth. "He must get back so that too many people won't know he's been gone. Mama, it's been like thirty years of growth since I left three months ago in March: I saw men die, blood shed, the craze of life in the big city, refinement and grace, the intrigue of palace and Temple, and—and much more!" Then Mary told how Zachary regained his voice and all the details of the birth of John.

"But tell me about yourself," asked Mama. "How is your baby?"

"All's well with both of us. Will tell you all after Aaron leaves. There'll be more time—here he comes now."

At the table Mary noticed that her mother was unusually loud with her chomping of the food. "Have you had trouble with your teeth, Mama?" she carefully inquired.

"Lost them all, three weeks after your father's death," and with the smile that accompanied that statement, she inadvertently revealed the fact. Her speech was noticeably altered with extra heavy sibilants.

"Poor Mama!" thought Mary. "She too is paying the fiddler." What a difference between here and Ain Karim. Her feelings raced from pity to affection. Was she finding it difficult to adjust to poverty? Was it the presence of Aaron, whose mind she was reading, that influenced her feelings? He was accustomed to things much better. The food they were eating was mostly dried, and the bread hard and stale. Would he go back and tell them what he had seen? Would they laugh?

"Why so silent, Mary?" asked Aaron. "How about opening some of those packages you brought for your mother from Ain Karim?"

"My mother—my home—thank God for both—" said Mary as she cleared the table and began the excitement of opening gifts—gifts from everybody, pieces of colorful fabric, interesting kitchenware, a rug, some choice foodstuffs, trinkets, and jewelry.

"Beautiful things. Beautiful!" spoke Anna. "But I'm always afraid of gifts for they might replace love."

* * * * * * *

Soon after Aaron's departure about noon the next day, Joseph came knocking on Anna's door. When he saw Mary, broom in hand, hair tied back, wearing an apron, his heart leaped. He rushed to her, and for a silent, timeless moment embraced her, lifting her and the unborn baby Jesus to the ceiling; then after dancing her about, he cushioned her face into his dusty beard. It was obvious he was glad to see her home.

Mary rubbed her nose and mouth attempting to wipe away the sensation of being feather-dusted, but she beamed all over at his enthusiasm.

"I didn't expect to find you here, Mary," said Joseph, "otherwise I'd have washed up. I came to do some work."

"No matter, Joseph—it's you—and I'm happy to see you."

During lunch Mary answered many of his questions, but in her womanly heart she couldn't help making comparisons. How much older he looked than Tobie. How unkempt his beard in comparison with that of Vitellius. How unrefined his conversation, unlike Aaron's. Still, there was a forthright manliness about Joseph, a wholesome naturalness which the others did not possess. He was unlocking the door to the chambers of her heart.

"Now that you're back, Mary," said Joseph, "we ought to move in together, the three of us, and into my place...."

"Yes, but what's going to happen to the olive grove?" asked Mary.

"Now that you're here, you and Mama can make that decision."

"Joseph, you are the man in this household," said Mary, "and I'm sure Mama and I will listen."

"Tell Mary about Simon ben Jonah," suggested Anna.

"Why, yes," said Joseph softly. "Simon offered Mama the deal that he would do all the work for two out of three bushels of olives. I suggested to Mama, and now to you, that you accept this offer, and in due time perhaps Simon will buy the property."

Before Joseph left that afternoon, the agreement was made between them that Mary was to move to Joseph's house on the first day after the next full moon, and Mama was to stay at the homestead until the day it was sold. At times Mary appeared anxious, and Joseph wondered why she was reaching out for his protection and care. He overrode any adverse thinking with the strong thoughts that soon she would be his and that perhaps the death of her father made her more dependent upon him.

As Joseph departed, Anna said, "I don't want you two to worry about me. Simon will take care of the olives—and I'll take care of myself."

* * * * * * *

In the face of personal challenges in Nazareth, time passed by swiftly for Mary. Work replaced worry, the present was more demanding than the future, and the constant presence of her mother was a happy diversion. Under the circumstances, she appreciated her mother now more than ever, her understanding and counsel.

"Why don't you take a walk over to the Hannans this afternoon, Mary," suggested Anna. "I'm sure you'll enjoy a laugh or two about the incidents of your journey to Jerusalem. Also, I think Deborrah needs a little cheering up."

"You won't mind, Mama?"

That afternoon, Deborrah and her spirited young daughters, Taman, Rachel, and Houle, were seated about the the outdoor table on the small patio, just outside the back entrance to the house. After the usual pleasantries, Deborrah asked if she could speak to Mary alone, so they went into the house.

"Mary, I hope you don't feel hurt," began Deborrah kindly, "but I've heard some awful things about you, which supposedly happened after you left me in the city. For one thing the townspeople are saying that you lived with a young man—must have been Tobie—in Ain Karim and that you were forced to run away with him."

"I lived at Zachary's every day after I left you, Deborrah. There was nothing else." She told her about how they nursed Tobie back to life, and how she and Aaron made a run for it to get home.

"I don't believe half of what I hear," said Deborrah, "but I did hear the girls talking about your condition. Are you expecting a baby?"

"I was pregnant when I left Nazareth with you," said Mary. "Why do people gossip so?"

"They're talking about me, too," consoled Deborrah. "They're saying I found a man in Jerusalem who is coming here for marriage. Some say that I've been secretly married."

"It's the devil," said Mary. "These people are guilty of murder, the killing of a person's mind."

"We're both on the public spit," said Deborrah. "If it gets too hot come and see me, and we can cry on each other's shoulder."

"Dear God," Mary prayed as she made her way home, "I know now how Miriam felt that night she jumped off the East Cliff. Abandonment. She was abandoned by everybody. Something good better happen to me pretty soon, or East Cliff may jump at me. It's bad enough to be stoned, but what's worse is to live in a hail storm. I can hear whispers all around me, their poking fingers, their hideous faces distorted with imaginary filth. But, God, since I'm not living with Joseph, and I'm not married, and I am pregnant, what can *we* expect?''

The next morning Mary made her usual trip to the village spring, still reeling from the blow Deborrah gave her the day before. Rebecca came. "Mary, it's all over town. I've heard it as often as I hear the birds. 'Mary found a new boyfriend. Mary is in love with a shepherd boy in Bethlehem.' Is it true?''

"What do you think, Becky?" asked Mary. "I'm glad they're not saying I married a rich merchant in the caravan, or maybe a Roman senator."

"It's serious, Mary," continued Rebecca. "They're wondering why you were gone for three months."

"I'll tell you, Becky, because you are a dear friend, and you'll believe me, but how can I tell everybody? They won't believe me."

"Evil prospers, and the good die young," said Rebecca. "You have told me enough, Mary. Let us pray that something good happens to you very soon." She swung her water pitcher atop her head, and said "See you. 'Bye."

Mary was alone, gazing at the swirling water. "How much evil would be averted if there were no public well. People wouldn't come here and gossip so much. You are powerful in your purpose and helpless in all else. Why can't each home have its own little spring? But what am I saying? I'm saying it about myself—my time has not come yet. It'll take more than water to wash clean the thoughts of Joseph; surely he must know what's being said. It's being said right in his own shop. He's getting only half truths. Someone must tell him the whole story. It's best that I be the one. Who else could?"

Mary passed Taman on her way home, the oldest and meanest of the Hannan girls. Neither one spoke. They felt sorry for each other but for diametrically opposite reasons—one a martyr, and the other the uncontrollable perpetrator.

"Mama! Mama!" cried Mary as she entered the house. "Where are you?" When she saw her in her chair, Mary dropped to her mother's knees. "My body is about to jump out of my skin! My mind wants to come out of my ears!"

"What happened?"

"I must tell Joseph, Mama. I cannot put it off any longer. He's got to know, now, today." Mary's tears flowed freely dropping into her mother's lap. With them went a confession of how many times she had thoughts of someone else; how she thought her mother and their humble home was not good enough; how she thought God had abandoned her so many times; how weak her faith was—and her love! "Mama, forgive me!"

"Your tears have improved your vision, my daughter. You now see your way more clearly, which you couldn't see before."

"I belong here, Mama. Do you think it's too late?"

"For God, it's never too late—nor ever too early. He is always standing at the heart, waiting for it to open. Yours has cracked open."

The next day was probably the longest day in Mary's life, as she waited for God's plan to reveal itself and for Joseph to come. She went over and over her long story she planned to tell him: right from the beginning when Gabriel brought her the message from God up to the moment when he danced her around with Jesus in her womb. The day indeed was long, but with sunset there began even a longer night, for Joseph never came. She surrendered—surrendered to hear God when the predawn-reflected light of the sun enabled her to distinguish the ceiling in her room from the walls that imprisoned her. She knew she belonged to God; she of all people knew what grew inside her. She believed.

From the Psalms she often spoke, she now found a line she could repeat: *"Enough for me, to keep my soul tranquil and quiet, like a child in its mother's arms after being weaned. . .rely on Yahweh, now and for always"* (Ps. 131).

She left her room that morning before dawn, found her way quietly to her mother's bed, and slipped in beside her. Mama startled a little, but realized at once her daughter had come home.

* * * * * * *

The mean Taman was at the village spring the next morning sporting for a willing ear to receive the latest gossip about Mary. Unfortunately for her, it was Rebecca whom she saw making her way up the hillside. Taman slid back into the dark recess of the enclosure to think it over.

" 'Morning," she said when Rebecca set down her pitcher. "Have you seen Mary lately?"

"Just the other day. Why?"

"Well, the latest is that she is expecting a holy child, one they say she conceived in the Temple, while she was in Jerusalem."

"A shameful lie!" said Rebecca.

"It was told to us by friends of my mother," insisted Taman. "They stopped yesterday on their way to Capharnaum. You know, they are Temple people, and it was there they heard it."

"The Temple is like a big community spring, a waterfall, where people gather from all of Israel for good and for bad," noted Rebecca. "You shouldn't repeat things like that, Taman. They're evil and will in time destroy you yourself."

"They said the father of her child is a famous Rabban, a friend of her cousin Zachary," the gossip persisted.

"You ought to be ashamed of yourself. Go home and bleed your tongue until it's dry."

"Has Joseph called off his marriage yet?"

"You just won't give up, will you?"

"I'd like to get to the bottom of it. Wouldn't you?"

"Snakes travel at the bottom, and you're one, Taman!" Rebecca swung her pitcher to the top of her head and moved off in a hurry.

* * * * * * *

The same cart that delivered the fresh load of diabolical rumors to Taman's mother had stopped at Joseph's carpenter shop for repairs on a damaged wheel. The owner of the cart lived in Magdala. He was sometimes called a merchant by his friends, but commonly described as a "rokel," one who moved from place to place peddling merchandise. Today he was practicing a corollary art, disseminating half truths, entertaining but vicious.

"Say," he said to Joseph, "I heard Nazareth mentioned quite frequently in the Temple area this last trip."

"Yes," said Joseph, engaged in solving the problem of broken spokes. "Nazareth is usually overlooked by the big city snobs."

"Well, what they are saying is a laudable thing: A young girl from Nazareth was in to see one of the famous Rabbans to tell him she was expecting to give birth to a prophet, or maybe the Messiah."

"Many young girls are making that claim nowdays," replied Joseph, chipping shavings off a piece of oak.

"This one sounds different," said the rokel. "She disappeared about the same way she appeared. They're looking for her. They think she is for real."

"I haven't heard of anyone making that claim here," said Joseph. "Your cart will be ready late this afternoon."

That afternoon, the man from Magdala started right in where he left off. "Say, carpenter, that girl I was telling you about, my wife says her name is Mary, a cousin of a priest, Zachary."

Joseph recoiled like he had been hit in the back with a javelin. "Mary, you say!" he exploded. "You must be the devil himself." He would not have heard this had he gone to Mary's earlier. "That's what I get doing this rokel a favor," thought Joseph. The news left him in a trauma. Mechanically he closed the shop, removed his leather apron, put it on a wooden peg, washed, took a second and third look at himself in a polished silver plate behind the door, combed his hair, fussed and fumed, but still couldn't get himself to go. It was growing dark rapidly.

"Too late" was now the excuse he spoke aloud. "That wandering Jew acted like he knew I had a personal acquaintance with Mary. How many people know this? The Hannans had something to do with this—that web-spinning black widow 'Taman.' " It was a long, long night for Joseph—and down the road a little, it was the same for the girl he loved.

Chapter 20

Joseph refused the chair that Mary offered him and kept pacing the floor from wall to wall. He knew he had to be here, but wished he were not for fear of what he might say.

"Joseph, please sit down and hear what I have to say," entreated Mary. "You don't know what you're doing."

"Did you know what you were doing three months ago?"

"Joseph, I want to tell you everything, but we must be calm. Neither one of us will make good sense unless we do."

"I'm the man here—I'll do the talking," he declared. "Is it true that you are expecting a baby?"

"Yes," said Mary softly.

"You are?"

"I was even before I left for Ain Karim—" Mary ventured to say a few words more.

"Who is the father?"

"The Holy Spirit. One week before I left, an angel, Gabriel, told me I was to mother a son, and his name shall be Jesus." She spoke too fast.

"Why didn't you tell me this before you left?"

"For some reason unknown to me, Joseph, I was afraid—but I'm not now."

"Why must I hear it from a rokel, and not from God—
or from you?" Joseph felt excluded. But he sat down.

"Papa was supposed to tell you, but he died," she
apologized.

"Why didn't your mother tell me?"

"She thought it would be better if I told you myself."

"Why didn't you tell me?"

"I'm telling you now."

"It's too late."

"Why? It's no different now than it was three months
ago. The fact remains unchanged. It's never too late with
God, nor too early. Joseph, I don't think you want to believe
me."

"Did the angel tell you how the child was to be
conceived?"

"Yes. He said the Holy Spirit would do it and the child
that will be born is the Son of God."

"Then did it happen?" The questions seemed forever.

"Then little Chometzla, a dark, little speck with a tail,
shone in the light, and it was all over." Mary wanted to
tell every detail.

"Had you told me all this when it happened, I would have
gone with you to Ain Karim."

"I don't think you were ready to believe me then, anymore
than you are now. I think God wanted me to do what I did
to help me grow up."

"I've heard there are many girls saying they're mothering the Messiah. Are you any different?" Joseph was running low on questions.

"I'll leave that to you to answer, Joseph."

"By all the laws of God and man, you belonged to me.
If God or anyone else wanted you, they should have spoken
to me first. It was my choice."

"Blame me, Joseph. I mishandled it—I'm truly sorry."

"I need time! Meanwhile, the public wedding we planned
is off—cancelled!" Joseph left the house (Mt. 1:19 ff.).

Being left alone with her unborn baby, Jesus, was getting to be a way of life for Mary. Even her mother separated
herself from "the lovers' quarrel" and listened in an adjacent room.

Mary retreated to her favorite spot, the window of her own room. She looked out at the animals in the corral. The old goat was down on his knees before his bowl of food, and his posterior was high in the sky supported by a pair of stiff and skinny legs, set far apart. Strange posture this for any of God's creatures, but not for an old goat, she thought. Hunger and a short neck taught him to bend his knees. "Joseph will learn, too," she said.

"Mary, are you there?" came the voice from the living room.

"Here, Mama."

"You've been in your room long enough. Come out."

"I really think Joseph believes I'm an adulteress, Mama." She came in.

"Maybe he's not thinking," replied Anna. "He's upset because he's not the father of the child."

"Mama, I can't get Miriam out of my mind—she seems to be calling me—I'm afraid to go by East Cliff...."

"That's all you need now—jump off East Cliff and make these Nazareans saints instead of gossip mongers, and then you will be one big liar."

"I guess when you're in my state of mind," said Mary, "the best thing to do is to go about your daily tasks and wait."

"The best advise yet. Let's just stop running and give God a chance to catch up with us," agreed her mother.

"I think I belong here with you, Mama."

"Your trip to Ain Karim has cured you."

"I'll wait and serve my God—waiting."

"At last," sighed Anna.

* * * * * * *

Rabbi Dock ben Zakkai, recently appointed to serve the people of Nazareth, sat across the table from Joseph in the synagogue seriously deliberating the alternatives in the case of the carpenter and the olive grower's daughter. "Joseph," he now concluded, "there are several ways of handling your problem. Before we get to that, however, I would urge you to set aside the arrogance of the executioner who stands beside his pile of stones prepared to cast them at the victim. Neither your accusation nor her claim has been substantiated in this house of God, and the self-righteousness you feel may be as wrong as the sin you condemn. Furthermore, even if she is found guilty, would you who presumed to love her now be the first one to throw the stone? (cf. Jn. 8:3). Our nation has been forgiven manifold times by Yahweh. Why can't we, His people, learn to temper justice with compassion?''

"I—I'm not ready to admit all that, Rabbi Zakkai," said Joseph.

"Very well, then," replied the Rabbi, "you are now ready to witness The Trial of Bitter Water as described in our Book of Laws'' (Nu. 5:11 ff.).

"Whatever." Joseph feigned indifference. "But," he added, "I hope it ends in a divorce, because I know I'm not the father!" (cf. Mt. 1:19).

"What you are asking for is called A Letter of Repudiation," said the young Rabbi. "This is a final settlement."

"Who notifies her?" asked Joseph.

"Nobody. This kind of thing is posted before the community and read aloud in the public square by the proclaimer.''

"That should be the end," declared Joseph.

"No doubt the end of the olive grower's daughter also."

"Ah—ah—is there—what was it you said about a trial?" asked Joseph.

"Yes," replied Rabbi Joch, picking up tempo. "You told me that you never claimed your rights of 'hakhnashah,' never lived with her, not as man and wife. Right?"

"That's right."

"Yet you swear that she left Nazareth for Ain Karim after she was pregnant."

"Why, yes, that's the reason why she left."

"If she didn't have hakhnashah with you, then who is the father?"

"I really can't believe it was a human," said Joseph in typical masculine logic. "We all knew her whereabouts every hour of her life."

"What's her explanation?"

"She was visited by the Holy Spirit who fathered her

child—this I could accept...if I had some sign, some proof—'' Joseph stood up and walked across the room.

"Our Law provides just that kind of proof—or disproof, if you will,'' explained the Rabbi. "It is prescribed in detail in the Book of Numbers and is called The Ordeal of Bitter Water. Are you familiar with it?''

"Never had any such experience. Does it prove that a person is lying?''

"—Or telling the truth! If she submits to the ordeal, your faith shall likewise be on trial. If she is innocent, you must believe.''

"Let's go ahead,'' said Joseph.

"Very well. Have her come in tomorrow morning.''

* * * * * * *

"I'm here to see Rabbi Joch ben Zakkai. My name is Mary, and this is my mother.''

"Kindly be seated,'' said the attendant, as he excused himself. He returned in a moment and invited Mary and Anna into a chamber which was already occupied by Joseph and the Rabbi. There was a quick exchange of glances, but strangely no one spoke, more out of awe than animosity. The Rabbi stood up and approached Mary.

"You are Mary,'' he said.

"Yes,'' she said, "and this is my mother.''

"In accordance with our traditions, there is a process described in the Book of Numbers called The Ordeal of Bitter Water which Joseph wishes you to take to prove your innocence. Are you willing to take it?''

"I am deeply grieved that Joseph doesn't believe me, but if my taking the test will bring us together, I'm more than willing to do it, and whatever else it takes.''

"I would now ask all three of you to come inside the Synagogue and take your places before the altar.''

The Rabbi stationed Mary directly in front of the altar and assigned seats to Joseph and Anna. He then procured a broad, low chalice, and placed it on the altar. Into it he poured water from an old algae-covered pot, obviously dirty, and after sweeping up dust from the floor around the altar, he brushed it into the chalice to mix with the stale water.

The Rabbi asked Mary to look at the chalice and meditate on its contents. Some Rabbis would describe the sickening ingredients of the dust which were at times found on the floor after country people had walked over it. Rabbi Joch didn't think it was necessary for Mary. While she stood in contemplation, he walked around her, unbound her hair, letting it drop as a veil around her. Next he took the barley meal offering from Joseph, placed it in her hands, saying this is an oblation for jealousy.

Then Rabbi Joch ben Zakkai returned to the altar, picked up the chalice of bitter water and, facing Mary, solemnly declared: "If it is not true that a man has slept with you while under your husband's authority, then may this water of bitterness and cursing do you no harm. But if it is true that you have gone astray...

> *May Yahweh make of you*
> *an execration and a curse*
> *among your people,*
> *making your thigh shrivel*
> *and your belly swell....*
> *[May it] shrivel your organs!"* (Nb. 5:11 ff.)

Mary responded, "Amen, amen," according to the ritual.

The Rabbi went to a nearby table and recorded the curses and their responses on an official scroll. He took the scroll to the chalice of bitter water and washed it. He now relieved Mary of the barley meal and, looking heavenward, extended it at arm's length, offering Joseph's gift to Yahweh. After replacing it on the altar, he took a handful and burned it, once again telling God that the offerer wanted to know the moral status of his wife.

Then came the time of truth. The Rabbi commanded straightforward: "Drink!" Mary first looked at Joseph; then without flinching, she placed both hands on the chalice and took not one, which would have sufficed, but several swallows. All waited anxiously. They looked for signs of nausea, or a faint. Mary remained as she was, firmly standing before the altar, her eyes fixed on the Rabbi.

The tableau was broken by the Rabbi when he turned to

Joseph and proclaimed: "The Ordeal is ended. There is need for no more." He stepped down to Mary and said, "I pronounce you innocent. You are free to go."

But Mary stood motionless. She was relaxed now, waiting for Joseph to come to her, to take her in his arms. She knew now more than ever that both she and Jesus needed him. She felt an arm slip around her waist and a hand touch hers. Secure—but, no, it was her ever-present mother. This time Mama's furrows were running with tears mixed with joy and sorrow.

Joseph had left.

* * * * * * *

War without spoils, victory without reward, Mary and Mama walked with arms around each other into the yard of their home, where Mary noticed tired-looking Alexander on top of the pigeon loft.

"News from Ain Karim, Mama. Let's go look!" To their surprise, they found that Alexander brought them two quills instead of the usual one. One was for Joseph. The other she opened immediately: *"All's well in Ain Karim. Zach's trip to the Temple settled matters in our favor. Baby John is fine. Love."*

"What shall I do with Joseph's note, Mama?"

"Take it to him."

"Right now?"

"Right now."

Up the hill and over the plateau went Mary to Joseph's house, hoping she'd never come back. The birds darted in and out in front of her, a lamb ran off to its mother, even the scraggy shrubs along the wayside rustled their branches and curtsied to her. She had love for all of them.

Joseph was in his workshop, an open-ended room facing the road. Someone was with him. "It's no more than a short ladder," she heard a man's voice protest. Joseph looked tired and annoyed. Mary stood quietly, awaiting her turn. "Bring it in," said Joseph, and the man left.

"Yes?" he asked Mary. He did not look at her.

"Alexander flew in a message for you." The quill was so small she held it in her open palm for him to take.

Joseph, smarting from the synagogue experience, was reluctant to reach in and touch Mary's hand, but because of that he fumbled and grabbed her hand with both of his. He managed to come up with the quill and began to fidget to get it open. She saw this meeting was closed. She slipped away to continue drinking in the refreshing consolations of nature. "He's as rigid as ben Hannan's sicas, and as confused as a jackal in Rome—I hope he doesn't hurt himself. Dear Lord, help him."

That night Joseph, the carpenter of Nazareth, the man God wanted, rolled and tossed in his bed like a pebble in the sea. The long nightmare wore on, spewing blackness around its prey. Strange voices seemed to fill the room from time to time, causing Joseph to call out, "Who are you? Who are you?" He couldn't tell whether he was awake or asleep. The feelings seemed to be the same now as they were in the afternoon. Was he in trauma, or willfully obstinate? Was it God or Satan? He had no way of telling.

The voices in his mind seemed clearer and closer. It was so real he could almost hear the High Priest call out the name of Mary, "This woman is innocent." A Rabbi came to his door—was it ben Zakkai or Zachary who stood in full ceremonial regalia? In his dream he left his bed to wrestle with the priest to take away the cup of wine he held that he himself might drink it. It promised strength and long life. He woke abruptly. Lighting a lamp, he went to the dresser and found the note that Mary brought from Zachary: *"Mary is innocent. Believe her. That which grows within her is of God. You are chosen to father both of them. Do not resist. Zachary."*

Once more he slept. An eerie voice pierced his slumber. "Don't believe a word of it! Mary is an adulteress. The child is not yours."

An authoritative voice said, "You know the child is not yours. And you know Mary is not an adulteress. What more is there?"

"Who are you?" Joseph heard himself demanding in his dream.

"Gabriel. Are you ready to listen?"

"Speak."

"Joseph, son of David, God directs you to be the father of this family, take them into your care. You shall personify the whole human race for he comes as the Son of God, conceived by the Holy Spirit to dwell among men for their salvation."

A brilliant light filled the room, and a mantle of peace enshrouded Joseph's mind. He was in the arms of God.

Gabriel said, "As a sign, you shall find Jesus, the Son of God, and Mary, God's favored one, completely submissive to your authority!"

"I am God's servant forever." Then he awoke. He was alone.

   "Here comes Joseph!" cried Mary as she pushed the goat
away and kicked over the milking stool. "Mama," she
gasped, "Joseph is coming."

   "Yes, I can see. It's not the first time he's come." Anna
wiped her hands in her apron.

   "But it's the first time I've ever seen him coming with
clenched fists. He's coming to attack someone."

   There was a hard knock on the door. Without waiting
to be admitted, in walked Joseph, his beard jutting out
straight from his face and his elbows flying. "Mary," he
declared, "I have come to take you home with me."

   Mary looked deep into his eyes, much the way she had
into Rabbi Joch's in the synagogue at the altar. Joseph
moved first.

   "The Lord has spoken," continued Joseph. "You shall
be my wife, and I shall father both you and Jesus."

   "Say no more, Husband." Mary stepped into the outstretched arms of Joseph and they held each other, trembling, rejoicing, fulfilled at last.

   "The festive day is now!" shouted Anna. "This calls for

some wine and music." Anna broke into a song and was joined by the others: *"Set me like a seal on your heart, like a seal on your arm; For love is strong as death, jealously relentless as sheol. The flash of it is a flash of fire, a flame of Yahweh himself. Love no flood can quench, no torrents drown!"* (Sg. 8:6). Anna poured the wine, clapped her hands to the rhythm of the song, and swirled with the others around the room. Tears rolled down her cheeks, she did not know whether from joy or sorrow, and cared less. But she did know that they were one family at last.

Joseph and Mary danced themselves right into the majestic armchair which was given to the head of the family, so Mary said, "Joseph, take your rightful position in authority right now." Then he spoke a line from the Song of Songs to hasten his lady on her way: *"Draw me in your footsteps, let us run. We shall praise your love above wine; how right it is to love you"* (Sg. 1:2).

Within the hour they were on their way. With a huge bundle of Mary's belongings across Joseph's stooped shoulders and with Mary carrying a basket beside him, they walked together over the long road home. They passed by the homes of people they knew so well. They saw them peeping out of windows; they felt their breath heavy with talk on their necks. They passed the home of ben Yochanan, the potter; Andreas, the freed Greek slave; Simon the retired fisherman; and Jacob the peasant—and then came the home of Jonathan ben Hannan. Taman was standing in the doorway, and in the windows were the others. Their laughter and talk was too far away to make sense to the young people going home.

"Mary, I owe you an apology," said Joseph as they drew near to the workshop.

"And I owe you one, Joseph," said Mary, "no doubt for similar reasons."

"Well, then, no explanations are necessary—let's make our beginning all even," he offered.

"All even...," mused Mary, "...even in love, in sharing, in waiting for our baby."

"Wait a minute there," he said. "*Our* baby is not exactly correct."

"God has given it to both of us," she explained. "I had not a man's love in its conception, no more than you had mine. Yet we both can share the human joys of expectation and growth."

"There's something to that," pondered Joseph. "Yours is the more difficult task—more difficult as the months go by...."

"I'll be mothering him, and you'll be fathering him day after day. I shall feed his little body, and you can develop his mind. I'll pray that he grows up to be a good man like you."

"You make me feel needed," said Joseph.

"Oh, Joseph—here comes Rebecca."

"She walks like her water pitcher is full," observed Joseph. "Let's not detain her."

"You two look like you're moving in," said Rebecca with a big smile of approval.

"Yes, finally," said Mary. "Don't forget to come and visit us."

"There's someone at the workshop," noted Joseph. "Wonder what's on his mind?"

"Are you the carpenter here?" the man asked Joseph. "Yes."

"A guiding handle on my plow is split badly. Can you make a new one?"

"Turn your back on your plow today, and come back tomorrow," said Joseph. He led Mary into the house.

* * * * * * *

Many villagers complained about the absence of the traditional week-long wedding festivities when they found out that Joseph and Mary had moved in together. Since they weren't forthcoming, some surmised that they must have been living together for a much longer time than was apparent. This is exactly what Joseph had been hoping for, since he knew that soon enough it would be physically obvious that Mary was with child.

A small town like Nazareth is easily distracted from a happening simply by another happening. People vie with one another to be first to tell about it. They let up on Joseph and Mary when Rachel, the youngest of the Hannan girls, died from an unknown fever. "She was so young," they said when they all turned out for the funeral.

It was only a month afterward that Taman, the oldest, married the village scallywag, who, like many a son of a Galilean, followed in the footsteps of his father, selling perfumes and fine fabrics. They said about him, however, that he bartered away the profits with his female customers for illicit services.

A beautiful relationship flowered between Joseph and Mary, personal and sympathetic. They shared a sense of destiny and felt their role in the promise of God through the prophets to send His people the Messiah. It couldn't have been otherwise, for without it Joseph would never have entered into the kind of "married life" he was enjoying with the very young girl, Mary. He realized the sacredness of the moment in history he was making at the command of the Master who commissioned his services, and from this flowed a disciplined and sublimated way of life. Still, he was human and at times the thought of having a son of his own became demanding.

Weeks became months, and months became a large abdomen for Mary, the carpenter's wife. One evening at dinner, Mary placed a sweet-smelling freshly baked loaf of wheat bread before Joseph, saying, "Papa, I hope you enjoy it."

"Papa?" exclaimed Joseph. "I never heard you address me like that before. You must be thinking of your own dear father, Joachim."

"No, I meant you, Joseph. Just a reminder that it won't be long before you see your son."

"God-given to both of us!" he said.

"How are you going to tell him who his real father is?" Mary looked tense.

"If he is what you say he is, I won't have to tell him. Nobody will. If he tells me who he is, I'll be scared to death. Someday 'Papa' and his 'Son' will have a good talk. How can it be otherwise? Truth shall free us all."

* * * * * * *

For a clergyman to visit his people was a waste of time, according to young Rabbi Joch ben Zakkai. He would rather call special meetings at the Synagogue and dispose of the people problems in one evening which otherwise would take him a week. Today, however, he made an exception and showed up at the workshop of the newlyweds, Joseph and Mary.

He found Joseph busy with a new contraption drilling holes into the seat part of a chair. "That's a real time saver, Joseph," greeted the Rabbi. "Where did you ever get it?"

"Comes from Egypt." Joseph proudly offered the Rabbi the bow and drill for closer examination. "It really works."

"Hmm, a very clever tool," observed the Rabbi. "Why couldn't a Jew have thought of that?"

"One of those things intended to increase our humility," said Joseph. "Please come into the house. Mary will be surprised and delighted to see you."

Indeed she was, and before Rabbi Joch had taken a chair, she had placed cakes, bread, and wine on the table in typical Jewish custom, offering the best of her larder to a visitor, and especially to her Rabbi.

"Surely you must have heard how restless the natives were," said the Rabbi, "when they saw that you two would not have any wedding celebration. Didn't you think it was necessary?"

"No," answered Joseph. "The Good Book allows us the right to move in together after our long engagement without fanfare. It is my privilege to claim my bride and bring her home for the Hakhnashah, the uniting of the husband and wife, the first night. This is all that is required."

"You are absolutely right, Joseph," agreed the Rabbi. "Our people were registering their disappointment. You know, a wedding can be more fun than a Passover celebration."

"Perhaps they'll think we've moved in together much longer—for the baby's sake," remarked Mary. No one commented.

"Another tale of woe has been brought to my attention," continued the Rabbi. "It is said that you are closely related by blood. Both of you are descendants of the family of King

David. How close is the relationship?''

"It is very far removed, Rabban," said Mary, "so far
that we can hardly enumerate the ancestry on one sheet of
papyrus.''

"Did I hear you call me 'Rabban,' Mary?" He was obviously pleased by the title.

"Yes.''

"Where did you pick that up? Certainly not in Nazareth.''

"Many people call my Cousin Zachary 'Rabban'.''

"I am flattered," said Rabbi Joch. "Did you ever meet
a real Rabban?" The question sounded naive, but Mary
responded.

"Oh yes; his name was Rabban Hammasiah, and he is
a member of the Sanhedrin.''

"Ah, wonderful," commented the young impressionable
Joch. "I've heard of him—a great dignitary. But let's get
back to Nazareth, to the purpose of my visit. As newly-
married people, you should be mindful of the laws and traditions governing the birth of a child into your family. First,
if the offspring is a boy, the mother shall be considered
unclean for only seven days. If it's a girl, then—''

"It's a boy, Rabban!" interjected Mary. "Tell us only
about the boy.''

"How would you know that?" asked Rabbi Joch.

"It better be; we have his name already—which reminds
me—the lamp.'' Even though it was the afternoon before
the Sabbath, Mary lighted the Sabbath-lamp on the small
table and poured more oil into it.

Dying in childbirth was a universal fear of Jewish mothers,
and Mary was no exception, so she observed the tradition
as directed in the Tractate Sabbath, which stated that those
who fail to light the lamp on the Sabbath would die in
childbirth. She would leave nothing undone for her unborn
baby.

"Now to get back to my admonitions," said the Rabbi,
"the boy, if you say so, should be circumcised on the eighth
day. Mother should then wait for forty days for her blood
to become purified, eighty for a girl—maybe next time—
before she attempts to enter the sanctuary or touch anything
sacred.''

Joseph was showing a little impatience, for he was hearing things he knew, and more than that, he didn't want to hear them now.

The young cleric's enthusiasm for pedantry carried him into the field of conjugal relationship in which he considered himself an expert: "Have you be instructed sufficiently in the duties of husband and wife in accordance with Chapter 18 in the book of Leviticus?"

"Yes, we have," answered Joseph, "and if you don't mind, we would rather not go into that at this time."

"I don't understand," said Rabbi Joch, "but it's your privilege since you already have a child—that is, a boy—on the way." He seemed to have run his routine with a newlywed couple for the first visit.

We thank you for coming, Rabbi Joch," said Joseph. "Perhaps we can have you stay for dinner."

"No thanks, not today. Maybe some other time." He made his way toward the door.

"Shalom, Rabban!" said Mary.

"By the way," added the distracted Rabban, "be sure to read chapter twenty-seven in Leviticus. It tells all about tithing. Shalom!"

Chapter 22

"Any change in the timetable, Mary?" Joseph put a few more sticks on the open fire in the courtyard.

"No. It's still the full length of 266 days, minus or plus eleven, as Yona told me five months ago." She tossed into the steaming pot a handful of chopped onion.

"If my arithmetic is correct, this being the end of October, we have nearly eight weeks to go, minus or plus eleven days. Right?"

"About 260 days after Papa's death," Mary reminisced, cleaning her hands on her apron.

Most Galileans marked time by events or natural phenomena, as after the last full moon, or so many days after the death of a loved one. From the rear balcony of the carpenter shop in Nazareth, Mary and Joseph had watched the golden wheat harvested in the plains of Esdraelon and the luscious grapes from the vineyards over the undulating hills pressed into wine. This year the harvests were somewhat damaged by the heavy rains blown in from the Mediterranean Sea, and it was cold and too often overcast. Twice they had hail.

Many of these days and nights were spent indoors where

Joseph and Mary literally sank their roots deeper into their native land and researched their ancestry: back to Abram they went and the land of Ur and then saw how he took himself a half sister, Sara, for his wife. They spoke of David's exploits and how he was their common ancestor.

One late evening in early December as Joseph and Mary were prepared to go to bed, he asked, "Do you think, Mary, that we should alert the midwife in Cana—what's her name?"

"Milcah," said Mary. "But why go to Cana? There are several here in Nazareth."

"I prefer Milcah from what I have heard of midwives."

A sudden sharp series of knocks resounded on the courtyard door, startling both Joseph and Mary. They both ran out, but he opened the door.

"Rebecca!" he cried. "Good to see you, but what brings you here at this hour?"

"Sorry it's so late," said Rebecca.

"It's not late, Becky. We were early in getting ready to retire." Mary softened the intrusion.

"I thought you should know—the Romans are making preparations to raise our taxes again—there's a bulletin on the Synagogue door that says: 'All peoples are to register in their native town.' Native town? That means Bethlehem, the city of David."

"Have a chair, Becky," invited Joseph, putting a chair under her. "—And how much time does the great Caesar give us?"

"The bulletin says thirty days."

"Thirty days? It's impossible," declared Joseph. "Mary has only twenty-one, plus or minus eleven. If I leave tomorrow, I'd hardly get back for my son's birth day."

"Go after his birth," suggested Rebecca.

"If I leave after twenty-one days, or it may be twenty-one plus eleven more or less, I'd be a few days late."

"No problem, Husband," offered Mary; "we'll go together—now, tomorrow."

Together it was. She had to pack things she had been making for the baby, long bands of cloth for swaddling, oil, salt, hand towels, pins, a bonnet, blankets, and of course diapers for Jesus. "I wonder if there'll be room for the crib Joseph just finished?" she thought.

"Now, Joseph, if you get the pushcart out of storage, we'll load up and be ready to leave in the morning."

"No pushcart on this trip, Mary. We're traveling light, and I'm going down to the Hannans and buy me one of those Lycaonian donkeys."

The next morning he heard Deborrah say, "All I have to sell you is this thoroughbred Muscat donkey, which you may know rides easier than the Lycaonian."

Joseph reached over the fence and rubbed the long grey ears of the friendly beast. "So this is all you have."

"You really don't want anything else. This animal is worth his weight in gold."

"Surely you're not asking that much?"

"Much less!"

"How much?"

"For rent, it'll cost you one shekel a month."

"That's three and half days' wages for a farmhand—too much."

"Then why don't you buy him outright!"

"How much?"

"Twelve shekels will take him home for good." The donkey's ears pricked up.

"That's forty-two days' wages for a farmhand."

"Farmhand maybe," noted Deborrah. "For a carpenter, it's a reasonable charge for good work. Look at him," she continued. "He has already bought you—he has his nose in your face."

"Tell you what, Deborrah," said Joseph, patting the sleek mane, "I'll make you a real sacrifice: two beautiful court-yard chairs and six shekels. You see, I can take shekels on the trip, but I can't take chairs."

"This muscat will travel twenty-five miles a day with all the baggage you get on its back." Deborrah was satisfied with the offer, but it wasn't the moment for grabbing. "Just feel the nice, shiny grey coat."

Joseph reached the same conclusion. "Deborrah, we had a nice visit. It is enough. Say it!"

"Take him away, Joseph, but I wouldn't do this for

anybody else."

"What's his name?"

"He's meant for you. 'Elon.' "

"Yes, that means 'Oak'."

"If he stops and refuses to move, don't build a fire under him!"

* * * * * * *

"Mary, we can't possibly get you and all those things on Elon's back," said Joseph. "It's not the weight; it's the bulk."

"Then I'll walk," she said.

"Then—you stay home!"

When he was out of sight, she returned some of her personal things with much difficulty, and the crib.

The first day of the journey was uneventful. It took them as far as Dathan. Midmorning the next day about seven miles south of Dathan, a sharp, sudden wind came up from the desert, a reverse current of air which originated off the Mediterranean. It was icy cold. Elon's instinct made him whinny repeatedly in alarm.

"It's a qadim!" yelled Joseph as he pulled in his cloak.

"Yahweh Sabbaoth, protect us," prayed Mary, not realizing that God had already started something in their behalf.

"The temperature will drop fifty degrees. We must find shelter. There must be a cave on the high side of that next elevation."

"I can hardly keep my balance up here," cautioned Mary, hanging on. "Mind if I get down and walk?" She took a position on the leeward side of Elon.

In early December westerly winds off the sea sometimes stack up against the hot wall of air over the desert and backfire with a vengeance into the west. The desert like a vicious monster blows back the balmy zephyrs or refreshing rain clouds, extracting what little heat they contain. The desert wants only heat.

The opening of the cave opened large enough for all to enter, even Elon, who immediately shook the chills out of his system. Mary began to clean up. Joseph thought he might build a fire, but the cold wind snapped through the opening, precluding a fire.

After a cold lunch, Mary sat off in the furthest corner, looking apprehensive. She was counting the days she had left before the birth of her child. "Today is our second day of travel," she thought, "so I have thirteen days to zero. If it's going to be eleven days less, then I have only two days before I enter into the period of possible."

"Joseph," she asked, "would you bring me a handful of pebbles?"

"Of course, but what for?" he asked as he left the cave. He was back in a hurry aided by a gust of wind. "Here they are, but why put a man into a qadim for pebbles?"

"I'm losing track of time, and the pebbles will help me. I plan to throw one away each night." She then tied them into a corner of her shawl for safe keeping.

Hours dragged on. The cold increased, and the sharp winds continued undiminished.

Then Joseph spoke what Mary was thinking: "We won't be traveling anymore today. We've got to stay here tonight. How do you feel, Mary?"

"Just fine, except that I'm cold."

"I'll get your heavy cloak for you. Where is it?"

"In the storeroom in Nazareth."

"—And yet I see you took all the baby bundles—we've got to do something about this." He left the cave.

He soon returned with an armful of juniper boughs found most everywhere in the hills of Samaria. He spread the boughs, maneuvered Elon to lie down so that his feet stretched out toward the opening of the cave, then had Mary lie next to him along his back, and finally laid down himself along Mary, tossing his heavy cloak over all of them. A moment of eternal silence passed. Only the snapping gust of the qadim could be heard. When Elon whinnied again, Joseph and Mary broke out in unrestrained laughter. They looked at each other and wiped the tears of tension away.

"I was wondering how I'd ever wash the sand out of my eyes," said Joseph.

Mary laughed aloud. She felt like a chick that had crawled back into her broken eggshell because of the cruel world outside. Here was the warmth of Joseph's body, and occasionally she brushed against Elon's hairy back.

As the light of dawn filled the cave, with it came the alarming sounds of gruff voices outside.

"Joseph," whispered Mary. "Wake up."

"What's wrong?" he said.

"Sh—sh—! Someone's outside. Listen!"

"What are they saying?" Joseph sat up.

"They are soldiers! They're saddling their horses. One seems very upset."

"What's he saying?" Joseph seemed disturbed himself for he wasn't hearing very well.

"I think he just called the king a bastard. Listen."

"That stupid Idumaean slave!" the soldier said. "He's got a lot of guts sending us up this rotten country in this qadim to find a pregnant woman."

Joseph started to crawl toward the mouth of the cave to improve his position. "Where is Elon?" he whispered.

"He left at the break of dawn," said Mary.

"He's probably grazing—far enough away, I hope."

Side by side, Joseph and Mary listened. They heard the soldiers say they were on their way to Sepphoris, the capital of Galilee, to enlist the services of the local police to make a thorough search for a young girl who is about to deliver what she thinks is a sacred baby.

"It is possible," said one of the soldiers, "that the child is already born."

"Herod, Hammasiah, and Company will never give up," said Mary as they heard the horsemen drive away.

"As the soldier said," repeated Joseph, "the murderous Herod sits upon a stolen throne and kills all competition." With that he took a handful of grain and went looking for Elon.

The last stretch of high ground for travelers from the north was Mount Scopus, from which Joseph and Mary beheld the awesome panorama of Jerusalem and its majestic Temple. The blood of their ancestors ran high with sentiment and faith, and for a moment they both thought they were on their usual pilgrimage to the Holy City. There always was the thought in the mind of every good Jew: "Next year in Jerusalem!"

Elon shifted his weight from side to side as he managed the rough terrain down the slope into the Kedron Valley. Joseph kept thinking: "Shall we take the chance and stop in the city to see the Temple? How much has been added to the reconstruction? Will Herod ever finish it?" The fork in the road ahead demanded a decision—to the right, Jerusalem; to the left, Bethlehem. Joseph halted. "How many pebbles did you count last night, *Mother?*" he asked.

"Well, thanks for the new title—you've never yet called me that" Mary was pleased.

"I remember when you first called me 'Papa.' Forgive me for not returning the compliment sooner. Anyway, how many?"

"Eleven."

"So we've entered the period of possible."

"Yes."

"It's not easy for a Jew to pass by the Temple without stopping. It grieves my heart," lamented Joseph. "It leaves me with an empty feeling. The kind we shall all have if and when the Temple is again destroyed."

"You mean like when our people were led into captivity in Babylon? I think the next destruction shall bring the greatest challenge ever to Judaism, the challenge to unite around a person rather than a building."

"It's something like this that the Messiah, the Son of God, will propose by his coming. The prophets all speak of it."

"Joseph, you said as much when you gave the Naphtir in Nazareth before I left for Ain Karim. Remember?"

"Yes, and it's more evident each day that something is going to break. All sects, all institutions are losing their identity. There is no confidence of people in their leaders, and Judaism is hit the hardest."

"Aaron thinks the son of Zachary, our John, shall cry to the high heavens for people to come to unity in the ranks behind a person."

"I remember your Cousin Elizabeth saying, 'Israel is heavily pregnant, and its pregnancy shall terminate with the birth of the Messiah, after which it shall remain sterile.' Harsh words! The Temple has failed."

"Not really," remarked Mary. "It has served its

purpose—and well.''

"You sound prophetic, but will you ever know?" wondered Joseph. "You sometimes amaze me."

"I'm not a prophetess, nor am I original," she explained. "I just listened well at Ain Karim."

As the Temple and the skyline of the big city faded into the background, his thoughts began to turn to more practical and mundane affairs such as shelter for the night. With the setting of the sun, a piercing chill settles upon the ground and makes man and beast uncomfortable. With Bethlehem now in sight, Joseph asked a passerby whether there was a caravanserai in the town. The answer was negative. It was much too small. He next proposed they stay at the Bethlehem Inn, near the edge of town. They found it overcrowded. They were directed to some limestone caves not too far distant which were used for animal shelters and at times by humans. There were many of these, formed by peculiar geological conditions of soft limestone layers interposed with horizontal bands of marl which were easily eroded by wind and rain. It wasn't so much a problem of finding one; it was rather a matter of choosing the best one.

"Well, Mary, this is home—for now." said Joseph, entering the wide-open cave. "Tomorrow, I'll try the Inn again."

A few rodents scurried out, and a bat winged its way into the twilight. "Come on in, Mary," beckoned Joseph. "I think we're alone now." He lighted a lamp and set it on a rock ledge. "I like the place because of one thing—it has a corner over which is a draft opening for a fire. Do you like it?"

"The place needs a lot of scrubbing," said Mary carefully. She went deeper into the cave, while Joseph carried out some of the dirt left behind by animals and humans. The lady of the house found a rickety manger, which she thought Joseph could firm up. Then she took a step back when she saw the rock formation on the opposite wall: The wall sloped down and toward her, dipping up a little about a foot from the ground. It had a small ledge on which she could sit, and two niches lower where she could brace her feet, "not unlike Yona's birthstool," she thought. She went over and sat in it.

"You've found yourself a comfortable spot," said Joseph

casually. "Stay right there until I bring in all our belongings and tidy up the new mansion."

Mary was lost in reverie.... "What else?" she wondered. "Joseph is here. There will be warmth, hot water—and God!"

Chapter 23

All the shepherds but one were gathered around the fire for the night, having left their sheep in sheltered ravines nearby.

"Tobie is long overdue," said one.

"It's not like him," said another.

"We're all here but Caesar."

"Easy, Haran," said a third, "we can do without the sarcasm."

The wind was hard off the sea with occasional rain and snow flurried, but mostly it was clear so that the stars appeared bright and glittering.

Out of the darkness stepped a young man, tall, lean, with a bearing of confidence and understanding. Some of his compatriots stood up. Haran, who competed for leadership at times, said, "Tobie, I have news that Sadduk is coming to Bethlehem; he'll be here before the moon is full."

"I have greater news," said Tobie calmly. "The long-awaited Messiah will be born this night. I was delayed to be given this information."

"How would you know that?" questioned Haran. "Give us a sign."

"Listen, sheep-counter—it's believers who are given signs! Unbelievers like you lose their voices, or their sight or something—"

Then the lights flashed, stars moved in the heavens, and voices filled the air. The men scattered behind rocks and trees and fell prone on the ground.

"Do not be afraid," said the clear voice of an angel. "I bring you news of great joy, a joy to be shared by the whole people. Today in the town of David a Savior has been born to you; he is Christ the Lord."

Nobody moved. Nobody spoke. Tobie was afraid Haran would.

"And, here is a sign for you," continued the angel, *"you will find a baby wrapped in swaddling clothes and lying in a manger."*

Then the shepherds joined the great throng of heavenly people and angels who were praising: *"Glory to God in the highest heaven, and peace to men who enjoy his favour."* (Lk 2:14).

About the same time, back in the humble surroundings of their new cave home, Joseph rolled over on his blanket in expectation of another night's sleep, when suddenly he heard the voice of Mary:

"Joseph!"

"Yes, Mary. I'm here." He sat up.

"Light the lamp!"

"Right away—has he decided to come?"

"Yes."

"I'll run to the Inn and try for a room."

"No, Joseph," answered Mary from the back of the cave. "Don't leave me."

"Here's the lamp," said Joseph, lighting it.

"Stir up the fire, and heat some water—and you'll find the baby's things in the manger."

"Right away!"

But first Joseph had to set down the lamp near Mary. As he came close to her, he noticed she was already holding the newborn Infant in her lap. He quickly picked Him up by His feet, swatted Him across the back, and listened to His strong, healthy crying.

For the next several minutes, the Joseph family was very busy. They were three now.

"It must be about midnight," said Joseph.

"I thought I heard the cry of a lamb outside," said Mary.

They listened. There it was, plus several more. Then there were human voices, voices of men, several of them.

The tall, lean shepherd stepped into the cave-home first, saying, "We are shepherds, come to pledge our loyalty to the newborn Savior—"

"Why, it's Tobie!" cried Mary. "How did you ever find us?"

"It was told to us from heaven," answered Tobie. He signalled his men to drop to their knees.

"We brought you sheep and goats, some dried meats, oil—Tomorrow we'll build you a corral, add a lean-to at the entrance, and leave someone with you to protect your property."

"Mary didn't say enough about you, Tobias," said Joseph gratefully. "Your generosity outdoes her enthusiasm."

The poot met in midnight darkness and left in the light of the world with a new kind of love prevailing.

After the guests had departed—and the wild noises of the nervous animals with them—Joseph returned to the cave, ready to take Mary into his arms in joyful celebration.

"Mary!" he called out in the darkness. "Where are you?" The crib was empty, and she was gone. "They must be outside," was his obvious conclusion.

Once again on the outside, he cried, "Mary! Mother and child, where are you?"

"Here, Joseph—" came the soft voice, not in panic or fear, but with a tone of finality mixed with joy and sadness.

"Where is here?" he called.

"Beside the big rock."

"You're crying," he observed. "What's wrong, Mary?"

"Joseph, will you take Jesus and hold him on your lap?"

Joseph took the Child and raised Him heavenward. "For our sakes a child is born to our race, a son is given!" (Is. 9:5). Then he embraced Mary and kissed her with tenderness.

She knew now he understood.

— NUNQUAM FINIS —